MESSAGE
in the
GRAVE

Message of Murder Trilogy Book 3

Dawn Merriman

Dedication

This book is dedicated to my wonderful husband, Kevin and my children. Thanks for all the hours of discussion on this book. Thank you to God for giving me the ability to tell this story.

-Dawn Merriman

Chapter 1

Gabby

If life is a roller coaster, I prefer the kiddy rides. The last few months have been a whirl of white-knuckle danger and sharp course changes. Hopefully, this consultation with my new client will be as easy as a trip on the merry-go-round.

The covered porch of the modest house protects me from the worst of the December snow, but a blast of icy air slithers down the collar of my coat. I pull the collar tighter on my neck and knock for a second time on the front door of Victor and Charlene Moony's home.

A large ball of orange fur sits on the railing. A dusting of snow coats the cat's fur and his bright yellow eyes watch me warily. "Hi, Kitty," I say to the cat. "Are your parents home? We had an appointment."

The cat continues to stare as I reach out a tentative hand to rub behind his ears. He leans into the pressure, rubs his cheek against my gloved palm.

"Looks like you're waiting for them too," I say,

wondering what kind of people my new clients are that they leave their cat outside in this cold.

A shadow falls across the cut class window of the Moony's front door and the cat jumps off the railing. The door flies open and an irritated woman barks, "What do you want?"

The cat slips inside the door and disappears.

I glance at the house number on the wall to make sure I have the right address. It's the right house, but the woman's rough greeting rattles me. "Uh, Mrs. Moony?"

"It's my house," the woman shrugs her heavy shoulders, "Now what do you want?"

"I'm Gabby McAllister," I say.

"So?" My name means nothing to her. Is that good or bad? Most people in town know who I am, at least by name. A recent media blitz about a case I solved destroyed any anonymity I once enjoyed.

"Your husband called and asked me to come look at an antique piano you own." I fish in my pocket for a business card and hold it out. She looks at the card in my hand but doesn't take it.

"My husband called you?" her eyes narrow as she scrutinizes my face. "Wait, I know you. You're that psychic lady everyone's been talking about."

"That's me. Is your husband home?" I pull the collar on my coat tighter.

Charlene Moony finally lets me inside the home, bellowing, "Victor, did you hire some psychic to look at the piano?"

After standing on the porch in the cold, the house feels

over-warm and smothering. Shelves dominate the room, each space filled with vintage items, knick-knacks, and an impressive glassware collection. A lovely old piano sits on display near the front door. There's no sign of the cat. I pull off my knit hat as a thin man enters the living room wiping his hands on a dishtowel. "Ms. McAllister, I'm so sorry. I lost track of time."

Victor offers me his hand to shake. Even through the gloves I always wear, his hand feels damp and hot.

"Is this not a good time?" I ask. "We can reschedule."

Victor shoots a look at his much taller wife and his eyes narrow a touch. "Tonight is perfect."

I'm new at this psychic-for-hire stuff, so I'm not completely sure how a house call should go, but this situation feels off. I plaster a smile on my face and use the voice I perfected as a phone order-taker for the catalog company I used to work for. Calm and professional with a touch of feigned interest. "Is this the piano you wanted me to look at?"

"That's my piano." Charlene places a possessive hand on the polished wood of the instrument. "Victor gave it to me."

"I see," I reply even though I don't. "And you wanted me to try and find out some of its history?"

Victor gives a long look to Charlene. She pulls her hand away from the piano and shoves it into her pocket.

"The history of it," Victor says, his eyes still locked on his wife. "Both the old and the recent."

Growing more uncomfortable, I'm ready to just get my reading done and leave. My chest grows damp from the

9

overheated room. I unzip my coat but leave it on. "As I explained on the phone, I might not be able to see anything, but my fee is the same." I pull a paper out of my inside coat pocket and hand it to Victor. "Payment must be made before I do," I look for a proper word. "My reading." I settle for the word most people are used to. I don't like the word, but it's hard to explain what I do.

Victor snaps the paper from my hand. "I understand. You take checks?"

"I prefer cash." I smile pleasantly to hide my irritation. I made it very plain on the phone, I only take cash. In this line of work, clients aren't always happy with the information I give them. Checks are too easy to cancel and credit cards can reverse charges.

Charlene watches nervously as Victor pulls the bills from his wallet and hands them over. I've seen her expression before. Most people grow uncomfortable around me once they know what I do. "What exactly are you going to be looking for? How does this work?" she asks curiously, not a trace of bellow in her now.

I pocket the cash and get to work. I've created an opening explanation to help clients understand what I can do and what I can't. Usually, I do readings at my shop on the square in River Bend and they bring the objects to me. I only agreed to this house call because the piano is so large. Maybe I should re-think my policy on house calls.

"When I was fourteen, I was hit in the head," I start my spiel, touching the scar on my eyebrow. "I was in a coma for three days. I woke up with the ability to sense things." I pause here, letting the information sink in. "I'm not

10

psychic the way you probably understand the word. I can't see the future or guess lottery numbers." Normally this line draws a nervous chuckle from clients. Victor and Charlene just stare at me. "What I can do is sense the history of items or people when I touch them. I don't know how it works or why I can do it. Sometimes I can't sense anything. I don't control the gift, but I try to use it to help people."

My explanation is meant to calm clients, but Charlene just grows more nervous. If I told her about the rest of my abilities, she'd really freak out. I don't tell clients about my cross tattoo and the messages it gives me. Only Grandma Dot and one other person know about that special talent. Only Grandma Dot still cares about me.

"I read all that on your website," Victor says. "Can we just do this?"

"Uh, sure." I pull off my left glove and approach the piano. Sensing things takes all my attention and leaves me vulnerable, and I'm always a little nervous. This crowded living room and the odd couple don't help. "Can you two stand over there while I do this?"

They move across the room as I sit on the piano bench. Sweat trickles down my chest, but the ivory keys are cool under my fingers. I close my eyes and open my mind. "Lord, let me see what I need to see," I pray so quietly the Moonys can't hear.

It takes a few moments for my nerves to settle enough to let the message in.

Passion, intimacy, sweat-slick skin.

I snap my hand off the keys in shock. "Crap on a

cracker," I mutter. "What was that?"

I look to Victor and Charlene in surprise. "What did you see?" Victor asks eagerly.

Charlene seems to shrink.

"I'm not sure," I say, but the guilty look on Charlene's face tells me all I need to know. "Let me try again."

The vision hits instantly.

Lovers in embrace, lust, desire, betrayal.

I slide my hand off the keys slowly this time. I came here to give my clients a lovely history of a treasured piano, not to destroy a marriage.

"You saw them together, didn't you?" Victor asks.

I nod, keeping my head turned away from the couple.

"I didn't do anything," Charlene tries to defend herself but gives her guilt away. She already knows, she was there.

And Victor suspected. "I paid for those lessons!" This time Victor bellows. "I knew you were sleeping with him. All those lessons and you never got any better at playing."

I slide from the piano bench, more than ready to leave. "I'm sorry," I stammer. "I told you I can't control what I see."

"You're lying," Charlene howls. My tattoo sends a sharp sting up my arm.

Duck.

I obey instantly and a ceramic statue zings past my ear and smashes against the front door. "Get out, you freak!" Charlene screams and a plate meets the same fate as the statue.

"You're the one who cheated," Victor shouts.

I pull the door open and dash into the cold night. The lovely glassware collection continues to shatter inside the house.

My cell phone is in my hand and Detective Lucas Hartley answers before I even step off the porch.

"You might want to send a unit over to Sycamore St.," I say by way of greeting. "I just exposed a cheating wife and the husband's not too happy."

"Good Lord, Gabby. You sure can cause trouble, can't you?" Lucas chuckles good-naturedly. As my brother, Dustin's, partner and lately my close friend, Lucas is familiar with my many run-ins.

"I don't cause the trouble," I protest. "It just finds me." Another loud crash carries across the front yard. "You might want to hurry on that patrol car. They're throwing things and I don't want anyone to get hurt because of me."

"Are you okay?" Lucas' always-ready concern for me settles my nerves.

"I'm fine," I say as I climb into my old Charger and start the engine. "Do I have to wait here or can this just be an anonymous tip?"

"You can leave. I'm only a few blocks away, I'll just check on them myself."

"I hate to make you go out in this cold."

"Happy for something to do. Olivia went back to her mom's last night, so the house feels empty."

"You're still coming to the party tomorrow night, right?" Just thinking about the party brings a wave of nerves.

"Wouldn't miss it."

I give Lucas the address to the Moony's and end the call. I snap my seat belt and pull it tight across my hips and chest. This consultation was a far cry from the kiddy ride I'd hoped for. On the roller coaster my life has become, all I can do is buckle up, hold on, and go along for the ride.

Chapter 2

Gabby

Icy air blasts against the floor-to-ceiling display windows at the front of my new shop, but sunlight pours into the room. The words stenciled on the window leave shadows on the polished but battered wood floor.

MESSAGES in large block letters with Psychic Investigations in smaller letters below and Gabby McAllister below that. Grandma Dot paid to have the windows lettered in shiny gold a few days ago. The bright display of my abilities and my name for anyone in town to see still makes my stomach quake.

With my gloves still on, I sit my coffee on the counter near the front windows and look around the room, making a plan for tonight. The counter, a remnant from when Grandma Dot had a beauty shop here years ago, is the only furniture besides a deep red couch and two yellow chairs that form a sitting area.

Before tonight, I need to get this space ready for a grand opening party. I gulp coffee to calm the nerves rolling in my belly at the thought of a crowd of people with their prying eyes and curious questions.

"Why did I let Grandma talk me into this?" I moan and lay my head on the counter. "I can't do this."

The cross tattoo on my left forearm sends the slightest tingle along my skin. "Oh, be quiet," I tell the tattoo.

A knock intrudes on my private misery. *Please don't be a client already.*

A familiar form fills the glass of the front door, and a different kind of tingle shivers through me. I open the door and Detective Lucas Hartley breezes into the room. His smile calms my nerves and he says the three words every woman longs to hear.

"I've got donuts." He sets the bag on the counter where my head lay just a moment ago.

"My hero," I exclaim, digging into the bag for my favorite cream-filled long john.

"Fresh from the bakery on the corner. Figured you'd be here this morning and could use a little encouragement," Lucas says.

"You figured right," I say, licking frosting from my upper lip. "I'm not sure I can go through with this whole thing."

My honesty surprises us both. "But you were excited about the grand opening before."

I swallow hard to clear my mouth of donut. "I know, it's just…"

"Now everyone will know about you?" He supplies.

I nod, feeling foolish.

"Everyone already knows, Gabby. At least this way you can control the message." He chuckles suddenly. "No pun intended." He points to the huge letters on the display window.

I roll my eyes, "Cute."

"Seriously, everything's going to work out. I have a good feeling about it."

"I don't." He focuses his dark eyes on my face.

"Did you…?"

I catch his meaning, "I'm just whining. I didn't have a vision or anything." I fill my mouth with donut to keep from saying more.

"The place looks great, by the way. I love the exposed brick and wood floor. Very like you."

"Dustin was afraid there'd be crystal balls and beaded curtains with incense burning. You should have heard him going on about it at Thanksgiving. My brother's such a tool."

This brings another smile from Lucas. "You've been through this with him before. He'll come around, he always does. He's coming to your party tonight right?"

I nod. "Dustin and Alexis. Grandma Dot and Mrs. Mott. My friend Haley from my old job. You."

"No Preston?" he asks, too casually.

I shake my head. "Pretty sure I scared him away. But half the town will be here." I roll my eyes. "Grandma Dot really got the word out about it. Might as well have put an ad in the paper 'Come see the freak in person. Tonight at 7:00'."

"It won't be that bad. It's only one night and you'll probably get a bunch of clients," he soothes.

"Hopefully better ones than last night. Using me to

17

prove your wife's a cheater isn't what I do this for. I want to help people." I look at Lucas pointedly. "I'm sorry I haven't started looking for your sister, Crystal, yet. I know it's not professional to say, but I have no idea where to start. I'm not very good at this investigation thing."

Lucas touches my gloved hand. "I'm a detective and haven't found a lead in almost ten years. You'll find something, I have faith in you."

"You won't hate me if I can't find out what happened to her?"

The heat from his hand penetrates the glove and warms my skin. "I could never hate you," he says seriously. The moment stretches and the air sizzles between us. This tension's become familiar in the last weeks. The confusion that follows is familiar as well.

I've known Lucas nearly all my life. First as the older brother of my grade school friend, Crystal, later as my brother's partner and friend on the police force. In the last several weeks, something in our relationship has shifted, indefinable. I pull my hand out from under his and sip my coffee.

I guide the conversation onto safer ground. "The rental company will be here in a bit with the tables and chairs and the caterer's coming this afternoon."

With his usual ease, he lets me change the subject. "I need to get to the station, but is there anything I can help with before I go?"

I look around my shop for anything I can't handle alone. "Not really. I'm just going to straighten up, clean the bathrooms, that kind of thing. I think I can handle it."

"There's not much you can't handle," he says. "Guess I'll leave you to it." He pats my hand again, and it lingers a moment longer than necessary. "See you tonight."

The bell on the front door jingles as it closes. The musical notes fade away, leaving a void behind.

"Grandma Dot, this dress only has three-quarter length sleeves," I exclaim.

Grandma smiles slyly and hands me the dark blue sweater dress. "It's going to look great with your blue eyes," she skirts my objection. "I'm not upset about the color," I point out. "My tattoo's going to show."

Grandma raises one shoulder, "So? Let everyone see it."

"I should have picked out my own dress," I grumble and pull the soft fabric over my head. We're getting dressed for my party in the apartment above my shop that I use as a break room. I trusted Grandma to pick out my dress, and I have nothing else here to wear.

"Too late now," Grandma says gaily, obviously proud of herself.

I look at my reflection and have to admit the dress fits perfectly and suits my eyes and dark curls. I tug self-consciously at the sleeve skimming just above my tattoo.

"Stop fidgeting. You look wonderful," Grandma soothes.

I pull the sleeve again, but the tattoo still shows stark black on my pale skin. "I feel exposed."

"Not exposed, revealed." She manages to make the words sound magical as she meets my eyes in the mirror.

"I don't want to be revealed," I grumble.

Grandma wraps her wiry arm around my waist the way she's done a million times before. "I know," she says simply and gives me a reassuring squeeze. "You look more like your mom every day," she says wistfully.

"I wish she could be here," I breathe.

"Me too," Grandma says sadly. "How did she seem at your last visit?"

"Tired and thin. That prison is slowly killing her. If I could just find Dad."

"We don't have time for that now," Grandma releases my waist and strides across the small apartment to another plastic shopping bag she brought with her.

"I bought you shoes, too." She hands me the bag with a grin.

"No heels, I hope. I don't want to fall down all night," I tease.

"Sensible flats for you. But did you check out my shoes?" Grandma shows off her sparkling strap-heels and short skirt. Grandma has two modes of dress. Comfy clothes are for working in her beauty shop or on the farm. When she dresses up, it's over the top with glittering accessories and too much skin showing. I envy her self-confidence.

"You look great, as usual," I say as I slip my feet into my sensible shoes. Below my flat-clad feet, voices fill the shop.

My belly swims. People, in general, make me nervous and crowds terrify me. My psychic gifts make me extra sensitive to the energy people give off, and I am easily overwhelmed by it. This crowd is in my personal space making it even more intrusive.

And they all came to gawk at me.

My belly clenches and I run to the bathroom, ready to vomit. I lean over the toilet, but nothing comes out.

"Just nerves, Gabriella. You're going to be fine, I promise." Grandma says, not unkindly.

I flush the unused toilet out of habit and watch the water swirl away, wishing I could swirl away myself. "I can't do this."

Grandma Dot pulls me from the bathroom. "You can do this. Now stand up straight and get your game face on. It's just a few people interested in what you do. That room down there is filled with friends and people who want to be your friend. Stop acting like you're headed to the gallows."

I do as she says, straighten my back and lift my chin.

"You've faced down psycho killers," Grandma goes on. "A room of nice people should be a breeze."

Should be, but isn't.

"You're right. I'm being ridiculous." I pull at the sleeve of my dress again, then run a finger along my tattoo. My fingertip tingles in response to the touch. The sudden surge calms me more than Grandma's words.

"Ready?" she asks.

"One more thing." I slide white dress gloves on. The fabric is thin, but provides some protection to my left hand from unwanted visions.

Grandma looks at the gloves and screws her mouth shut.

21

"Not negotiable."

Grandma gives me a quick hug and says, "Let's go meet your new life."

Chapter 3

Gabby

Slowly lowering myself down the stairs, I'm amazed at the transformation to my shop. The bare brick walls and sparse furnishings have changed into a softly lit wonderland. Strings of white lights drape along the walls, casting a soft glow. Several narrow pub tables with matching stools dot the room. The old counter is now a chic wine bar. A buffet table laden with hors d'oeuvres sits near the door.

"You've outdone yourself," I whisper to Grandma Dot as we reach the bottom of the stairs.

She beams with pride, "Mrs. Mott set it up. Her nephew owns a catering business."

"It's lovely," I say in awe.

The packed room teems with people. Some I recognize, many I don't. I hesitate on the steps, looking for Lucas. He catches my eye from near the wine bar and nods.

My friend, Haley, joins me as I enter the pressing crowd. "What a turnout," she exclaims.

"Why are they all here?" I ask honestly. "Nothing else going on in River Bend tonight?"

"Right now, you're the hottest thing to ever happen in River Bend," Haley says. "Enjoy it. You deserve this."

Lucas appears at my side with a glass of wine.

"Almost as good as donuts." I take the glass eagerly. Haley taps my toe with hers and raises one eyebrow a fraction of an inch. "Oh, yeah. Lucas this is my friend, Haley. We used to work at the catalog center before I got myself fired."

"Nice to finally meet you, Detective Lucas," Haley purrs, her already pretty face flushing as Lucas shakes her hand.

"Hey, Haley," I cut in. "Can you go make sure Grandma Dot has a glass of wine?"

Haley drops Lucas' hand reluctantly. "Sure thing. Hopefully, we can talk later," she adds with a toss of her long blond hair and a coy smile.

Lucas smirks, seeing through my ploy. "Is that the friend who calls me 'hot detective?'"

"Of course, you'd remember about that. You're so full of yourself," I tease. "Haley's my friend."

The press of the crowd forces us together and Lucas says near my ear, "Your friend that you just sent away from me." His breath dances across my ear and the nape of my neck tingles.

"Don't read too much into it," I reply, his body mere inches from mine.

The crowd presses around us, but their presence fades to a dull din. Lucas' eyes cling to mine and I swim in the scent of him.

A hand clasps onto Lucas' shoulder and the moment shatters. "Hey, Hartley, can I steal you away from my sister for a minute?" Dustin shouts above the noise of the crowd and steers Lucas away.

Although surrounded by people, I feel alone and wish I hadn't sent Haley away. Tugging at the too-short sleeve of my dress, I wander through the crush towards the bar. This party just started, but I wish it was over already.

In the far corner, Grandma Dot chats with a few ladies I recognize as clients of the beauty shop. I envy her easy manner, sure her belly isn't dancing with nerves the way mine is.

No one actually stares, but I catch a few side glances in my direction. Like an animal on display, I lean against the front counter and smile at the pretty red-head serving drinks.

"Nice party," the bartender says kindly. "Are you having a good time?"

"I feel like everyone's staring at me," I tell her honestly and take a sip of my wine.

"You are kind of popular right now," she says. "Drink some more wine. It'll make you feel better." The bartender smiles again. "It's really good," she adds. "Made it ourselves."

"You must be married to Mrs. Mott's nephew who catered for us."

"That's right. I'm Vee Markel. Lane and I own the Kingston Winery and we do catering as well."

I take her advice and sip the wine again. "It's really

good. Vee? That sounds familiar," I muse, trying to pluck the woman's face and name from my memory.

"We went to high school together," Vee supplies, tucking a strand of her brilliant red hair behind her ear.

"That's right." I can't pull up a clear memory of the woman. I spent most of my time in high school alone, trying to remain unnoticed, avoiding the ridicule of being the psychic girl with a mother in prison.

Vee's easy smile disappears as she looks behind me.

I turn at a tap on my shoulder. "Ms. McAllister?" A middle-aged woman asks shyly.

"You can call me Gabby," I correct automatically.

The woman is so thin, her huge pile of permed curls looks like it might topple her over. "I was wondering if we could hire you." She motions to her companion. The other woman sports a similar over-teased perm and the resemblance of mother and daughter is instantly recognizable. The daughter hangs behind her mother's shoulder, obviously uncomfortable.

"Sure, what can I help you with?" I turn on what I hope is professional charm.

"I'd like you to speak with my father." The woman states simply. "He died several years ago, and I …" Her voice breaks with emotion. The daughter stares at the floor.

"You'd like to know that he's okay?" I fill in the words for her.

"Exactly," she says with relief. "Is that something you can do?"

"I can try. I never promise anything. I don't control

what I might or might not be able to see."

The woman's hair bounces with her excitement. "That's okay. I understand. I'd just like to try."

"Can you come tomorrow morning so we can discuss the details?"

The woman looks at her daughter. "We can do that. Can't we, Lucy?"

Lucy would rather be anywhere other than here, now or tomorrow morning, but she gives in. "Sure," she mumbles to the floor.

"Do you have something of his you'd like me to touch?" I ask.

"He's buried in Haven Crest Cemetery. Can we go to his grave? Would that work?"

"I've never tried it, but I'm willing. We can just meet there, at the front gates. Is nine o'clock a good time?"

"Perfect," the woman gushes. "I'm Annette Reed and this is my daughter, Lucy." Lucy doesn't lift her eyes from her intense scrutiny of my wood floor. Her mother reaches to shake my hand, but makes a last-moment detour to rub her palm against her own thigh. I've seen this move before and don't take it personally.

Plucking a business card off the pile on the bar, I hand it to Annette. "Please visit my website before tomorrow morning so you know what to expect," I say politely.

"Oh, I've already been on there lots of times," Annette gushes. "You're amazing, just amazing."

Her reluctance to touch me, I'm used to. The open praise I'm not used to. Luckily, Haley appears at my shoulder, saving me from replying. "Grandma Dot says its time for you to make your speech."

My blood freezes. "A speech? Is she nuts?"

"Looks like you're in demand," Annette says. "We'll see you in the morning."

I make a vague reply to the mother and daughter, my eyes darting to the front door. Maybe I can run away before Grandma Dot notices.

"Here," Vee the bartender says, "Liquid courage."

I take the offered wine glass and down the contents. Grandma Dot is sailing through the crowd towards me. Unaccustomed to drinking alcohol, the wine swims in my head along with the adrenaline pumping through my veins.

"Ready?" Grandma asks.

"You never said I'd have to give a speech," I protest.

"What do you think all these people are here for? They want to hear from you."

My legs wobble as Grandma pulls me through the crowd to the stairs. "I can't. You do it. This party was your idea."

"Nonsense," Grandma brushes my protests away. "Just get up there and thank everyone for coming. Tell them what you can offer as a service. Then say, enjoy the party and contact me if you want to hire me." Grandma squeezes my arm gently. "It's easy. I'll introduce you."

We push through the crowd, bodies jostling against mine. "Okay, but give me a minute."

Near the bottom of the stairs, I close my eyes for a moment and take a deep breath. A hand grasps my bare arm, covering my tattoo. I catch a whiff of a familiar cologne and a shock sizzles up my arm. One word pumps through my mind.

Dad.

My eyes fly open, but I'm surrounded by bodies. Grandma Dot stands on the third step, the facing crowd pressing closer, eager to listen. I look for the person who touched me, but everyone's attention is on Grandma and her words that I'm not listening to.

"And here she is," Grandma says, "Gabby McAllister."

The attention shifts to me.

"You're up," Haley says near my ear.

"Did you see who just touched me?" I ask, desperate.

"Don't worry about that now. Speech." Haley gives me a little shove up the steps.

My mind scrambles to find words as I join Grandma above the crowd. "Uh, thank you all for coming," I stammer, scanning the crowd for a face I know can't be here.

Dozens of curious faces look up at me. My tongue refuses to move.

Grandma whispers in my ear, "Just tell them about yourself."

I rub my tattoo nervously, then begin the spiel I use on clients. "When I was fourteen, I was hit in the head…."

As I speak, I scan the crowd. Every face I either recognize, or know I've never met them before. The buzz of my tattoo grows and I tug at the short sleeve of my dress. Somehow, my mouth keeps moving and the words tumble out. The crowd chuckles at the lottery numbers line and I relax a little.

Near the bar set up by the door, a man has his back to me. His turned back in the sea of faces watching me is enough to make him stand out.

The familiar shape of that back freezes my tongue.

A nervous ripple flows through the crowd at my sudden silence. The man moves to the door, then looks over his shoulder.

A thick beard hides most of his face, but his brown eyes are unmistakable, unforgettable. He nods slightly, then slips out into the cold. The bell above the door jingles as he leaves.

"Dustin, it's Dad!" I shout across the crowd. "He's getting away." I point to the now empty door. Every head in the room turns. I bolt down the steps.

"Move! I have to stop him from leaving," I shout at the startled crowd, pushing people out of my way.

I rudely shove my way to the front door, Grandma Dot trailing behind me. Calling, "Gabriella, what in the world are you doing?"

Dustin and Lucas get to the door before I do and I shove them outside in front of me. "I saw him! He was just here."

Cold air blasts up my sweater dress as we tumble into the dark.

The sidewalk and the town square are empty.

I sprint down the sidewalk, desperate to find him. "Where did he go?" I shout into the icy wind.

At the corner, near the bakery, I stop running, scanning the streets, the square, everywhere.

"He's gone," I pant into the wind. "He was just here."

Grandma, Haley, Dustin, and Lucas join me at the corner.

"What the hell are you up to?" Dustin barks. "Jesus, Gabby. Dad?"

"I promise. I saw him. He touched my arm and then I saw him go out the door."

The four people closest to me in the world look at me with varying expressions of pity.

"Maybe today was too much on you," Grandma says gently, steering me back up the sidewalk.

"I…." I don't know what to say. Shame and embarrassment burn through me as I shiver in the cold.

Lucas awkwardly pats my shoulder. "I'm sure you thought you saw him, Gabby."

Dustin storms ahead of us, grumbling, "I knew this was a bad idea. Officially your Grand Opening and you've already managed to embarrass the family." Dustin reaches the small crowd outside of my shop. "Nothing to see here," he says like the cop that he is. "Miss McAllister just had a momentary excitement. Everything is fine now." He ushers the onlookers back inside.

Miss McAllister? He's really ticked.

I want to go home, climb into bed with my cat, and forget the last five minutes ever happened. But I have a room full of people to deal with first.

"Do you want me to say something to the crowd?" Grandma asks as we re-enter the party.

"No, I've got this."

Without a trace of nerves now, I climb back up the steps and face my confused future clients. I can't make a bigger fool of myself now than I just did. My business and my livelihood are at stake.

"Whoo," I start. "Sorry about that." I give the crowd a wide smile. "You may have heard I'm a bit, what's a nice word for it? Crazy?" A nervous ripple of laughter. "I think the wine we're serving is a little too good." Chuckles now from the crowd and I know it will be okay. "Vee," I motion to the bar, "Get the wine flowing, and let's get this party started." Vee holds up a bottle, playing along. "Thank you, everyone, for coming tonight and enjoy."

I hurry down the steps and say to Grandma, "Was that okay? Everyone likes wine right?"

"You did fine, Gabriella," Grandma soothes. "Do you want to tell me what that was all about now?"

I shake my head, "Not tonight. Maybe it was just too much wine."

Grandma narrows her eyes. "Uh-huh."

"Go back to your friends and have a good time."

Grandma reluctantly disappears into the crowd, leaving me alone with Lucas and Haley. "Wow, Gabby, never a dull moment with you," Lucas says.

"I try. Can we just pretend it never happened?" I ask them both.

"Let's get something to eat. Mrs. Mott's nephew did a great job with the food," Lucas says and leads the way to the buffet table.

Haley taps my elbow as she follows. "Uh, Gabby?" she tucks her hair behind her ear nervously. "I saw the man you were talking about."

"You did?"

"He had a beard and wore a leather coat?" I nod. "He brushed by you right before your speech."

Chapter 4

Gabby

I'm glad I set my appointment with Annette and Lucy Reed at the cemetery instead of at my shop. After last night's humiliating run down the sidewalk, I'm in no hurry to return. The party turned out okay, all things considered.

Dustin left early and hasn't returned the apology voice mail I left him this morning. Not sure what to say to fix that situation anyway. Lucas and Haley kept me company most of the night and their acceptance makes up for Dustin's anger.

The vents in my Charger pump stale heat into the car as I sip my coffee and watch the snow falling on my windshield in the cemetery parking lot. I have five minutes until Annette and Lucy are supposed to meet me.

If they still show up. Publicly making a fool of myself isn't the best way to impress a new client. I drink my coffee and wait, wishing I'd eaten something for breakfast.

At two minutes till nine, a car pulls into the parking lot. Annette waves animatedly as she approaches, her full perm bouncing. Lucy trails behind, her chin tucked into the collar of her puffy coat.

"Crap on a cracker, they actually showed up." I down the rest of my coffee in one gulp, wincing as it hits my empty stomach. "Here we go."

"Oh, Gabby, I'm so excited," Annette practically squeals. "I've missed my dad so much since he died."

Mention of fathers makes my cheeks warm against the cold air. "I hope I can see something for you," I say sincerely. "I can't promise what I'll see. I don't control my gift," I remind her.

"I know. I read that on the website. Here's the payment, by the way." She hands over the cash eagerly and I quickly push it into my coat pocket without counting it.

"Are you excited, too, Lucy?" I ask the quiet woman. The daughter seems surprised to be spoken to directly.

"Oh, she's ecstatic," Annette answers for her. "Been chattering on about it all morning."

Lucy looks at the snow-covered ground, and I can't imagine her chattering about anything.

"He's right over here," Annette continues, leading us into the cemetery.

A chill that has little to do with the cold slithers down my back. As a rule, I avoid cemeteries, but my new business venture will probably lead to more readings like this. I hunch into my coat collar and focus on the job I came here to do.

It doesn't take long to find Annette's father's headstone. The granite sparkles in the pale sunlight and nearly fresh flowers flash their bright colors against the thin snow. "I brought those a few days ago," Annette says.

"They're lovely," I mutter absently. Every inch of my skin begins to tingle as I near the grave. It feels like ants climb under my clothes. I resist the urge to itch.

"What do you need us to do?" Annette asks.

My head swirls and her words are hard to make out. The itching ants grow stronger. "Shh. Just stand there quietly," I command.

My tattoo stabs my arm, cutting through the growing haze in my mind. The sudden, unbearable pain knocks me to my knees. Snow melts into my jeans, the bite of cold ground a distant annoyance, overridden by the pain in my arm and the tingling of my skin.

"Gabby are you okay?" Annette's high voice comes from miles away.

I can't stand and drop both hands onto the grass covering the burial plot of Annette's father. On hands and knees, my chest clenches.

I can't breathe, I can't breathe. Lucas, please. Mint and vanilla smothering. Air, I need air. Lucas!

Annette and the now-speaking Lucy shout my name. Their voices barely pierce the vision.

Betrayal, pain, disbelief. I can't breathe! I wasn't going to tell. I promise I wasn't. Don't do this. Mint and vanilla, cloying perfume. The chain from my necklace cuts

into my neck. Lucas' necklace. The beautiful bird
pendant. Air, I need air.

"Gabby, oh my God!" Rough hands pick me up from the grass of the grave and the vision breaks.

Annette tumbles backward, the weight of my limp body pressing her into the ground. I scramble away from her hands.

"Don't touch me!" I scream inconsolably. "I can't breathe."

"Gabby, it's Annette," she calms. "I'm not touching you and you can breathe. Just breathe. Just breathe."

I open my eyes to a pale white sky, snowflakes sinking lazily to land on my wet cheeks. Annette and Lucy stand over me, watching with worried expressions.

"What happened?" I croak, my throat sore.

"I don't know. You fell down and then started writhing around and crying," Annette replies. "Did you talk to Dad?"

I push myself into a sitting position, confused and dizzy. "Your dad?" I ask dumbly.

"That's Dad's grave. Did you see something from him?" Annette seems as confused as I feel.

I shake my head violently, trying to make sense of what I saw. "It wasn't your dad," I say slowly. "I saw Crystal Hartley."

"Who's Crystal Hartley?"Annette asks.

Lucy has her back to me and she stares at the grave. Her tall perm bounces and her shoulders shake as she cries. I must have scared the timid woman.

"A girl I once knew. She was murdered. Call the police

station and ask for Dustin McAllister. Only Dustin," I tell Annette.

I can't talk to Lucas right now. Not after living through his sister's murder. Not when her dying thoughts were of him.

I dig the cash out of my pocket and shove it at Annette. "I'm sorry. I can't reach your dad. He's here, but Crystal is in the grave, too. I won't be able to reach him."

"Keep the money," she says gently. "You earned it."

She returns the bills, then explains to the 9-1-1 operator that she needs Dustin.

I need Lucas. But how can I trust him now?

I huddle on the snowy grass, shivering with cold and emotion as I wait for the police. Annette walks Lucy back to their car, then returns with a blanket. She wraps the blanket around my shoulders, then sits next to me.

"I'm sorry," I tell her, wiping my running nose on the back of my gloves.

Annette hands me a tissue. I'm amazed at the change from a nearly-giddy girl to a caring adult. Must be a mom thing.

"You don't need to be sorry. That must have been terrifying." Annette stares at her father's headstone. "Maybe I needed to bring you here. Maybe Dad was trying to tell me something. I just had to come with you and try. You know what I mean? He knew she was here and wanted you to find her."

"So you believe me?"

"Of course I believe you. You're Gabby McAllister."

I give a humph of disdain. I'd rather be anyone other than myself right now.

"So you knew this Crystal girl?" Annette asks wrapping her arms around her knees.

"We were friends in middle school but drifted apart as we got older. She's the sister of my brother Dustin's partner." Dustin's partner, not my friend, or more. Apparently, I know Dustin's trick of distancing.

"Dustin the detective I just talked to?"

"The same. His partner, Lucas, asked me to find out what happened to her. She ran away right after high school and no one has heard from her since. I guess we know why, now." My nose continues to run and I swipe at it angrily.

"This Lucas isn't going to be happy with what you found. I don't envy you that conversation."

Annette doesn't know the half of it.

Lucas didn't kill her. There has to be another explanation.

I rub my gloved hands hard against my face. "It's definitely more complicated than that," I say, then shove my lips tight together. I will not tell this odd woman what I saw, no matter how nice she's being to me right now.

I won't tell anyone about Lucas' possible involvement until I know for sure.

"Was she nice?" Annette asks.

I've thought a lot about Crystal in the last few weeks. Images of her as a kid flash through my mind now. Us swimming in her above ground pool during the summers. Riding our bikes to get ice cream on the town square.

Whispering about the boys we liked and the girls we didn't like until all hours of the night.

"Yes, when we were friends, she was very nice."

All the early memories shine bright and pure. Attached to each of them is Lucas. Her big brother always on our periphery, sometimes annoying, sometimes welcome.

The later memories, after I nearly died and woke with my abilities, don't shine as bright. Slowly, but increasingly, Crystal pulled away. Our sleep-overs ceased and she no longer invited me to swim. It wasn't long until she was hanging out with other girls, sleeping over at their houses. Staying up all hours talking. I became one of the girls she didn't like and spent many lonely nights wondering if she whispered about me behind my back.

Even here in the cold, that thought burns my cheeks. I'd loved Crystal and she'd deserted me after I became a freak.

And then she was gone.

And it took a freak to find her.

Chapter 5

Dustin

The crack in the ceiling above my desk stares back at me as I lean in my chair and study the ceiling. Gabby's voicemail re-plays through my mind as I think. She'd sounded honestly sorry about her crazy antics last night. I want to believe her, want to forgive her.

Why can't she accept Dad is dead?

A disturbing thought niggles at the back of my mind. As much as I hate to admit it, Gabby is often correct. Doubting her hasn't worked out so well for me before.

I sit upright in my desk chair and pull my keyboard closer. The desk facing mine is empty, Lucas' desk. I shoot a quick look around the squad room, but no one pays me any attention.

I type Nathaniel McAllister into various search engines, both public and law enforcement. No records, except the ones related to his murder fourteen years ago. The only recent mention of him from a parole hearing for our mom, Emily McAllister over a year ago. She remains in the women's prison near Indianapolis. Nathan

McAllister remains dead.

I shove the keyboard away impatiently. *Damn it, Gabby, now you have me searching for ghosts.*

The ringing of my desk phone intrudes on my grumpy mood.

"Detective McAllister, a woman is calling in and will only speak to you," dispatch says.

My mood sinks from grumpy to plain angry, "Is it my sister?" I bark. *Really, calling dispatch because I won't answer your voicemail?*

"It's another woman, but she says she's with Gabby," dispatch replies with just a hint of enjoyment at our family drama.

I sigh heavily, "Put her through."

"Detective McAllister," a high, thin voice. "I'm Annette Reed and I'm at Haven Crest Cemetery with Gabby."

I grunt in response, tapping a pen on the desk in irritation. A cemetery? Probably cavorting with dead relatives.

"Gabby says to tell you she found Crystal Hartley."

My tapping pen freezes.

"What do you mean?" I brace for the answer.

"Apparently, she's buried in my father's grave. Gabby sensed her."

Crystal Hartley? Holy crap, what will Lucas think?

"We'll be right there."

"Only you," Annette Reed says quickly. "She said only you can come."

Rubbing the rising tension in my neck, I look at Lucas'

empty desk. My partner and friend has been searching for his sister for ten years. Finding her dead will crush him.

Pulling on my coat, I hope Gabby's wrong about this.

But Gabby's rarely wrong.

An impossibly thin woman with large hair waves animatedly across the cemetery. My boots crunch on the thin snow as I plod past headstones, looking for Gabby. I find her huddled on the snowy ground near the excited woman. Her head rests on her bent knees, her arms wrapped defensively around her legs.

"Can you believe it?" Annette Reed bubbles, her manner a sharp contrast to Gabby's forlorn figure.

Gabby doesn't raise her head from her knees, piquing my irritation. I scan the marks in the snow. Three different sets of footprints mar the white surface. Near the headstone, several smudges of yellowed winter grass peek through the snow.

A set of handprints show clearly on the grave. Gabby's handprints. I shudder.

I find Gabby eyeing me warily after I inspect the scene. "What happened?" I ask.

Gabby opens her mouth, then shuts it again. Annette answers for her.

"We came here so Gabby could talk to my father. He died ten years ago, and I miss him so much, you see."

I just nod at the odd woman.

"Well, when we walked up, Gabby fell on her hands and knees. She started crying and shaking. We had to pull her off the ground. To stop the vision, I guess."

"We?"

"My daughter is here, too." Annette motions to the parking lot. "She's waiting in the car."

Gabby searches my face as Annette explains. "I'm sorry," she finally whispers.

"What did you see? Are you sure it's Crystal?" I ask carefully.

Her eyes narrow a touch and her shoulders stiffen. "Of course, I'm sure."

I glance back at the disturbed grass of the grave. Nothing seems amiss to my eye.

"She's buried there. On top of Annette's father." Her voice louder now, stronger. "She was murdered." Her eyes slide away from mine and drift over the cemetery. She's hiding something.

I shuffle my boots in the snow. *What do I do with this information?*

Gabby supplies an answer, "You'll have to exhume her. Lucas and his family will want to give her a proper burial." Her voice catches on Lucas' name.

"I can't do that," I snap bluntly. "I can't exhume a grave because of a hunch you have."

She jumps to her feet in anger. I prefer the anger to the forlorn form I first encountered. "We both know it's not a hunch. I saw her. I saw the necklace Lucas gave her. I saw…." Her mouth snaps shut on the last part.

"I'll give permission," Annette ventures. "It's my father's grave. I'll allow you to…," she searches for the word. "To get the girl out," she finishes awkwardly.

I kick at a pile of snow. "I'll still need a court order. I

won't be able to get one."

"You have to do something," Gabby pleads. "It's Crystal. You can't just leave her here."

Rubbing my neck does nothing to relieve the mounting tension. I blow out air in exasperation. "We'll have to talk to Lucas," I finally say. "If Crystal really is here, he has to know."

Gabby turns pale and resumes her scan of the cemetery. "Can you tell him?" her voice tiny in the cold. "I don't think I can."

"He'd rather hear it from you," I point out.

Her eyes lock on a distant point, "I can't," she says simply.

A tense silence stretches between us.

"Do you need me to give a statement or something?" Annette asks to break the silence.

"No," I sigh. "There's nothing to report yet."

This earns me a sharp look from Gabby, just as I planned.

"Go home," I tell both women. "I'll handle it."

Gabby turns on her heel and strides away without a backwards look or word, leaving me alone with Annette.

"You must be very proud of your sister," the thin woman says. "She's really something."

I manage to keep the sarcasm out of my voice, "Yeah, she's something."

Annette's eyes narrow and her mouth scrunches. She heard the sarcasm after all.

Chapter 6

Grandma Dot

After Gabriella's stunt last night at the party, her name is on the tongue of every client at the beauty shop. The grand opening party was intended to get the town talking about Gabriella's services. People are talking, alright.

"Do you think she really saw Nathan McAllister last night?" I'm asked for the umpteenth time this morning. "Isn't that exciting?"

In the reflection of the wall of mirrors, I lock eyes with the woman who asked the question. "We've already been over that. Whoever Gabriella thinks she saw last night, Nathan is dead." I give the woman a withering look. Even my tiny black dog, Jet, stares at her from under the counter near my feet. The woman waits for her color to set, and will be here for a while yet. Better stop her tongue wagging now.

She looks down at her magazine and away from my glare. I resume the hair cut I'm giving to Anthony Aniston. I run my shop on walk-ins only, and a if a man stops in for a quick trim, I try to get him done and out the door. The women like to hang around and visit, the men just want to get back to work.

"I hear Lacey's got an interview with the NBC affiliate in Indianapolis," I say to Anthony to shift the suddenly tense mood in the shop.

"She did, yesterday," the proud father beams at me in the mirror. "Said it went well. Lacey's worked hard to get her reporter career off the ground. Hard to do in a town like this where nothing exciting ever happens."

My scissors freeze over his short, unruly curls. "Nothing except stopping a serial killer and taking down a cult." I point out. I leave out the part that Gabriella is the only reason Lacey's career is going anywhere. Lacey's whole angle has been to make Gabriella look bad. But if it means Lacey might move to Indianapolis, it's a small price to pay. "She did great on those stories," I lie through my clenched teeth.

From her usual chair in the corner, Pauline Mott ineffectually covers a laugh with a fake cough. I dart my eyes to her through the mirror and she coughs again.

Anthony Aniston doesn't notice Mrs. Mott. "Both our girls are doing so well for themselves, aren't they?" he says.

I snip the last curl, resisting the urge to take a chunk of hair from the back of his head where he'll never look. "Yes, they are," I reply politely, setting my scissors on the counter and brushing the loose hair from his shoulders.

Anthony stands up and pulls some bills from his wallet. I put the bills in the money drawer and don't offer him change. "Thanks for working me in so fast," he says.

"Anything for you, Anthony." I smile, letting him think I did him a special favor. I motion for a woman with rollers in her hair to take the empty chair.

"You have a nice day, ladies," Anthony says to the room, in the tone of a man who expects all women to be sad when he leaves.

"Bye-bye, now," Mrs. Mott says sweetly.

The bell on the door jingles as he shuts it behind him. Mrs. Mott's laugh joins the jingle.

"Stop that," I chide my best friend and begin removing rollers from my next client.

I only have six rollers out when the door jingles again and Jet barks. "Oh my gosh, Dot, you won't believe it." Annette Reed blows through the door, stomping snow on the mat in her excitement. Her daughter, Lucy, trails behind her, morose and silent as usual, Jet sniffing at her feet.

"If this is about what happened last night at the party, she's not interested," the woman I silenced earlier says.

"Last night?" Annette asks, scanning the room of women. "Oh, yeah, that." Annette pulls off her coat and tosses it on the only open chair in the shop. "No, this just happened."

Fear swims through my belly and I pull out the next roller from my client a little too hard. I mumble an apology to her and ask, "What happened?"

"Gabby found a dead woman," Annette states without pre-amble. "In the cemetery."

"The cemetery is full of dead people," Mrs. Mott

51

points out.

"Not like this. There's a murdered woman buried in my father's grave." Annette looks around the room, basking in the attention.

A ripple of interest flows through the room and a sinking feeling flows through me.

"Who?" the woman with half the rollers still in her hair asks from my chair.

"Some girl Gabby knew from school. Crystal something or other."

A few gasps escape from hanging mouths. "Crystal Hartley?" Mrs. Mott asks quietly.

Annette nods, her tall perm bouncing. Lingering by the door, Lucy stares out a window.

My mouth suddenly dry, I drop another roller on the counter then usher Annette through the sliding pocket door to my kitchen. The shop twitters behind me.

"Tell me what happened?" I demand in the quiet of my kitchen, scooping Jet into my arms.

"Gabby went with us to the cemetery to talk to Dad. You know?"

I nod.

"As soon as we got to his grave, she fell on the ground and started crying and carrying on." Annette looks over her shoulder as Mrs. Mott quietly joins us. "She was really gone. I pulled her off the ground and she came back to the present. She was so upset, saying she couldn't breathe."

Annette runs a hand down her face. "It was the most amazing thing I've ever seen," Annette's eyes glow with awe. "She found her, can you imagine?"

"Did you call the police?" Mrs. Mott asks.

"Your grandson came. Dustin. He said there's nothing we can do. The dead girl might not actually be there."

"Dustin's like that," I grit out through clenched teeth. "There wasn't another detective with him? Lucas Hartley?"

Annette shakes her head. "They talked about him, but Gabby didn't want to see him."

The bad feeling in my stomach congeals. "You haven't told anyone else have you?"

Annette shuffles uncomfortably. "I came straight here," she evades. "Anthony Aniston was in the parking lot just now."

I blow air in exasperation. If her dad knows the story, Lacey will soon be on Gabby's case with camera in hand, demanding the next big scoop and flinging accusations.

"Annette, do me a favor," I say gently, ushering her to the back door. "Please go home and keep this to yourself."

Annette seems confused, "But isn't this exciting?"

"Things usually are where Gabriella's concerned," I reply. I gently shove her towards the back door.

"Oh, Lucy's still in the beauty shop," Annette hesitates.

"I'll send her out to you," Mrs. Mott says, blocking Annette.

"Well, okay then." Annette opens the door. "You'll let me know how it all turns out, right?"

"Of course," I soothe. "But this is a matter for the

police now. The best thing we can do is keep the details to ourselves."

She nods solemnly. "A matter for the police," she repeats.

"Thank you for understanding." I shut the door behind the woman and take a deep breath. "Our girl's gotten herself into something again," I say to Mrs. Mott.

Her pale purple poof of hair bounces as she nods in agreement. "What are you going to do?"

I look out the window at the back parking area of the farm. "I'm surprised Gabriella hasn't come here," I muse.

"She's never found someone she knew before. Maybe she needs some time alone," Mrs. Mott says practically.

"She needs her family," I state firmly.

I turn the open sign to closed and finish up the last few clients waiting in the beauty shop. No one asks about Annette's sudden announcement and Mrs. Mott steers the conversation into safer waters. With one ear on the driveway, listening for Gabriella's roaring Dodge Charger, I put the finishing touches on the last client.

"Well, it's time we went," Mrs. Mott says to the woman, a not-so-subtle hint that I need them to leave. The client hurries into her coat and out the door.

I bundle Jet in my arms and stare out the window at the empty driveway. "Where is she?" I ask Mrs. Mott.

"Go find her," she replies, patting Jet on the head. "Call me later and let me know she's okay." Mrs. Mott wraps a scarf around her pale purple poof of hair I expertly set this morning.

"You're good to her," I muse.

"She's a good girl."

As she leaves, a dusting of snow blows in the open door and settles on the chairs in the waiting area. I tuck my nose into Jet's fur and stare at the snow, yearning to hear the Charger. As the snow melts to water droplets before my eyes, apprehension melts into my blood.

"Wanna go for a ride?" I ask Jet.

Gabriella's driveway is empty, her small house sad in the snow. I try her phone again, but she still doesn't answer.

"Where could she be?" I ask Jet. He wags his tail and puts his feet on the window of my flatbed truck, recognizing the house. "She's not there," I tell him. He pants excitedly, not understanding.

We sit in my truck, snow falling gently on the windshield. I'd already driven past her shop and all the lights were out, no car parked in its usual spot in the alley. I don't know where else to look.

The wipers swipe at the snow, a forlorn sound fills the cab of the truck. Desperate, I close my eyes and lean my head back on the seat. Gabriella gets her talents from my side of the family and I've always fancied myself a bit gifted as well. Nothing like her abilities, just a sense of things that I shouldn't have.

With my eyes closed, I open myself to that sense now. Listen to universe, hoping for a sign of where to find my granddaughter.

I don't hear a location, but I put the truck in drive and

make my way through town. When I feel the need to turn, I turn, to go straight, I go straight. I push conscious thought away and drive on instinct.

I find her gray Charger parked at the cemetery. Leaving Jet in the warm cab of the truck, I pull my knit hat over my ears and step into the silence of falling snow. Far across the sea of gravestones, I see her.

A lonely figure huddled against the cold.

The angle of her shoulders stiffens as I approach, but she doesn't turn.

"How'd you find me?" she asks.

"I have my ways." I take her gloved hand in mine, squeeze it in reassurance. "Is this where you found her?"

She sniffles in response.

"I'm so sorry. I didn't want you to start your business so you could be upset." I say the guilty thought that's plagued me all morning.

"It's not your fault. It's his." She sniffles again.

"I don't follow."

"Lucas. She was thinking of Lucas as she died. She begged him to help her, to stop."

The gravity of her words knocks speech from my lips. We listen to the snow fall for a few moments as my mind reels for how to respond. "You know Lucas didn't have anything to do with her death," I finally state firmly. "There has to be another reason."

"A reason she was thinking of him as she died?" she snaps. "There's only one reason."

"Lucas did not hurt his sister." I grab her by the upper arm and shake her. "Lucas has been your friend nearly all your life. He's been the one person to stand by you. You cannot believe he'd do anything like that."

She snaps her eyes at mine. The anguish swimming there makes me drop her arm. "I saw it. Watch."

She suddenly pulls off her gloves and drops to her knees in the snow. She places both bare hands on the cold grave. Her body shakes and bucks from the vision. "Lucas, please," she cries, "Lucas."

Watching her receive the vision terrifies me. I know what she does, have seen it happen before, but never like this. "Lucas, please," she begs again from deep in the vision, her body shaking with emotion, her hands gripping the grass and snow.

"Stop that!" I scream in horror, unable to watch her torture herself. I wrap my arms around her waist and pull. A shock of fear and the smell of mint and vanilla fills my senses, Lucas's name whispers through my mind.

We roll onto the ground, both of us gasping. My chest hurts and my senses sting. "What the hell was that?" I say to the gray sky.

"That was Lucas murdering his sister," she says miserably, climbing off me.

She retrieves her gloves from the ground, slides them back on, then reaches to help me up. For the first time in my life, I hesitate to touch her, even with gloves.

I avoid her the slightest sliver of a moment, but she sees. Her face crumples in pain and betrayal. "Get away from me," she screams.

I scramble to my feet and throw my arms around her. "Gabriella, I'm so sorry," I say into her tight shoulder. She tries to wriggle away, but I wrap myself tighter around her tense frame. "I love you so much. I'm so sorry."

Shame swamps me as I cling. "You flinched," she sniffles near my ear, her voice muffled by our coats.

"I know." The truth, only the truth can fix this. "I saw what you saw, and I was scared. Not of you, but of the…." I don't know how to finish the sentence. "I'm never afraid of you."

"You flinched," she says again, miserably, but her body softens and her arms pull me tighter.

"Shh," I soothe. "Everything's fine now." Confident she won't pull away, I run one hand over her hair.

"What am I going to do?" she begs into my shoulder. "What will I tell Lucas?"

I put her at arm's length and meet her miserable eyes. "There's no way Lucas killed her," I say as evenly and clearly as possible.

"But, you saw it too."

"She was thinking of him, but that doesn't mean he killed her. There has to be another explanation."

Gabriella cocks her head sideways as if listening to a voice far away. Her face settles into resignation. "I have to talk to him. I owe him that much."

She suddenly throws her arms around me again and kisses my cheek. "I love you, Grandma Dot."

I watch Gabriella walk across the snowy graveyard. Shame still simmers in my soul. Cold bites at my nose and cheeks and my fingertips sting. I deserve the small pain.

Chapter 7

Gabby

Grandma Dot's tiny slight stings me to the core, but her embrace and desperate pleas of loving me cool the burn. If she truly did see some of what I saw, I can't blame her for freaking a bit.

She seems so sure of Lucas' innocence. I should have such faith. Her words in his defense give me courage, but the tingle of my tattoo telling me to go to him sets my feet in motion.

Once in my car, I call him. His "Morning, Gabby," greeting when he answers stabs my heart. He sounds so happy, so relaxed. I hate to ruin his day, ruin his life, but I owe him the truth.

"I need to talk to you," I say.

"I must be popular. Dustin just said the same thing to me."

"Don't talk to him," I snap suddenly.

"Why not?" he questions, his voice filling with

apprehension. "What's going on?"

"Where are you?" I hedge.

"At the station."

"Just wait for me. I'm only a few minutes away. Don't talk to Dustin until I get there, okay?"

"He's right here. Are either of you going to tell me what this is about?"

"Just meet me out front." I hang up before he can push the issue and pray that Dustin keeps his mouth shut.

Both Dustin and Lucas wait for me in front of the small police station. Dustin wears an expression as gray as the overcast sky. Lucas leans against a light pole, attempting to appear relaxed. The attempt fails. I know him too well.

My heart stings as I watch him. My feelings for Lucas are complicated and confusing, especially now.

I park at the curb and approach on dragging feet. Dustin glowers, "I thought you said…."

I cut him off, "I know what I said. But I have to do this myself."

Lucas looks from my brother to me. "One of you want to clue me in here?" Agitation tinges his words.

"I've got this," I say to Dustin.

"Have it your way," he grumbles. "You always do."

Lucas watches his partner's retreating back then turns his weary eyes to mine. "It's about Crystal, isn't it?"

Now that I stand in front of him, my doubts fade away. This is Lucas. My friend, my maybe more than a friend. No matter what I think I saw, Grandma Dot is right. There has to be an explanation that makes sense.

"Can we go somewhere private?" I hedge.

Lucas looks up and down the deserted sidewalk. "It's pretty private here," he grumbles, growing annoyed with my evasion.

I stare at the cracked and snow-dusted concrete, unsure what to say. "I found Crystal," I finally blurt out.

"You did?" he exclaims. "Where is she?"

The hope in his voice nearly shatters me. "She's...." I trail off, wishing I could blow away with the cold wind. "She was murdered." I say plainly.

Air rushes out of Lucas and he leans against the light pole for support. Another officer exits the station door and glances at us curiously. "Can we sit in my car?" I offer.

Lucas follows numbly.

Once inside the car with the heat blasting on our faces, I start my story. I explain about Annette Reed and why I was at the cemetery. Despite the heat in the car, my teeth chatter as I reach the part about finding Crystal.

Lucas stares out the window and down the street as I talk. Once I finish, we sit in silence.

"You're sure?" he asks miserably.

I don't bristle at his doubt. "I'm sure. I even went back and checked again. She's there. Has been all along. The date on the headstone coincides with when she ran away."

"She didn't run away," he says flatly. "She was taken away from us."

His pain is a palpable thing in the enclosed car. It rolls off him in waves. Real pain and shock, not faked surprise from a killer. I hate myself for ever doubting him.

"There's more." My words barely audible over the

blasting of the heater. I fiddle with the knob and turn the blast down.

He turns to me, searching my face. "You know who did this, don't you?"

I pull at the cuff of my coat, fingering a loose thread nervously. "Not exactly."

His eyes plead for answers.

"She was thinking of you."

He looks as if I slapped him. "What do you mean?"

"Her last thoughts were of you. 'Lucas, please,' to be exact."

"Why me?" pain etches his face, settles into the creases at the corners of his eyes.

"I don't know. But that's what I heard."

He spins suddenly in his seat. "You thought I did it, didn't you?" he accuses.

I pull hard on the loose thread at the cuff of my coat. It breaks off in my hand. "I don't now."

"But you did," he snaps. "Jesus, Gabby." He runs his hand hard across his face. "You told Dustin? You didn't call me right away." He looks back down the street. "You thought I killed my own sister?"

"She was thinking of you," I try to explain. "I didn't know what I thought. I was pretty shook up at finding her there."

Lucas pulls hard on the door handle and slams the door open. "You know, Gabby," he looks directly in my eyes, the intensity making me flinch. "You and I have been through a lot together. Never, I mean never, have I doubted you. It'd be nice if you showed me the same courtesy."

My mouth opens, but there's no protest I can make. He climbs into the cold and slams the door behind him. The whole car shakes with the force.

My whole body shakes as I watch him stalk away from me, leaving a yearning hole at my core.

Exhausted and hungry, I drive through town yearning for a sandwich or taco, or anything to fill the emptiness inside. "Crap on a cracker," I mutter, noticing the time. Food will have to wait. I'm late for another appointment with a client.

I pull into my usual parking spot in the alley at the shop and let myself in the back. The outline of a person darkens the glass of the front door. I hurry to let my client in.

"So sorry I'm late," I chatter as I pull the door open. "I had another appointment and it went long."

"Another appointment? Is that what you call it?" the blonde woman snides.

Lacey Aniston's impossibly white teeth and perfectly applied makeup greets me.

"You're not my next client," I say dumbly, a sinking feeling settling into my empty belly. "What are you doing here?"

Lacey pushes her way into the shop. At least she doesn't have a cameraman with her. Not yet. "I heard about your little find this morning. Thought I'd get the scoop straight from the source."

"You know I'm not going to tell you anything," I reply, holding the door open. "You can leave now. I'm expecting someone."

Lacey ignores the open door and inspects my shop. She huffs at the scuffed wood floors and lifts her chin high in disdain. "Nice place," she says sarcastically.

I swing the open door in invitation, "You're letting the cold in. Please leave now." I fight to keep my tone even.

She continues to ignore me, so I close the door.

"So you just happened to find Crystal this morning," she says leadingly. "You two used to be friends, didn't you?"

I don't justify the implications with a response.

"Now you're dating her brother." To my horror, I feel my cheeks burn.

"Lucas and I aren't dating."

Lacey shrugs and tosses her long blond hair over a shoulder. "If you say so. A little coincidental that you, and only you, knew where she was buried."

My hands ball into fists and I yearn to pummel her surgically altered nose. "Get to the point, Lacey. I'm too busy for this."

"My point is that you two were friends, then you weren't. That had to sting. Then Crystal was murdered. Only you knew where to find her. It doesn't take a genius to connect those dots."

"You're certainly not a genius." I'm gratified to see her fake smile droop at the insult. "To answer your ridiculous question, I didn't have anything to do with Crystal's death. I only found her by accident."

"Coincidence and accident. Sure."

My fist takes on a life of their own and I raise my hand

to strike.

A knock at the door saves Lacey from my attack.

I lower my hand and force my fists to open. "That will be my client," I say through clenched teeth, "Now get out before I throw you out." I open the door to a surprised woman.

"Lacey, what are you doing here?" Ashley questions clutching a plastic bag to her chest.

I'd forgotten that Ashley and Lacey were friends. I hadn't seen them together since I found Lacey's lost son a few months ago at the superstore. That feels like a lifetime ago now.

"I could ask you the same thing," Lacey says to her friend, eyeing the plastic bag Ashley clings to.

"I…." Ashley stammers, her face pink from cold and embarrassment.

"It's none of your business what my clients are here for," I snap at Lacey. My hands ball into fists again and a headache starts pounding above my left eye near my scar. Lacey finally gets the point and looks at my hand.

"I'm watching you Gabriella McAllister."

"Enjoy the show," I say and shove her as gently as I can through the front door.

Ashley stands guiltily in my shop once Lacey is gone. "I'm sorry about that," I soothe. "I didn't know she would be here."

Ashley uncrosses her arms and lowers the plastic bag to her side. "It's okay," she says vaguely.

My stomach grumbles and my head pounds mercilessly. "Look, Ashley, I'm sorry to do this," I say rubbing at my scar. "I've had an awful day and I'm afraid I'm not up to doing the reading you want today."

Ashley looks down at the bag in her hand. "I understand." A faraway look crosses her face. "It can wait. Can we reschedule?"

The tension in my shoulders slips away in relief. "That would be wonderful. I want to give you my full attention, and I'm afraid I can't offer that right now."

"Tomorrow then?" she asks hopefully.

I'd rather put it off for a few more days, but I agree to tomorrow.

Ashley hesitates at the door, "What did Lacey want with you? She didn't want to hire you did she?"

I laugh out loud at that. "We both know Lacey would never pay me for my services. She'd rather use me to make a name for herself as a reporter."

Ashley has the good grace not to gossip about her friend, only looks at the floor with a sly smile.

"She heard about something I found this morning and was trying to get a story out of me."

"What did you find?" Ashley asks, genuinely curious.

"I'm sorry, I can't tell you," I say politely.

"Oh, of course. Of course," she mutters.

"I'm sure it will be on the news tonight, knowing Lacey. Most of the details will be blown out of proportion, but that never stops her."

Ashley smiles prettily at the floor again and reaches for the doorknob. "See you tomorrow?"

"I'll be here."

I lock the door behind her and breathe a sigh of relief.

The roller coaster has started again and I'm sure a wild ride is coming.

But first I need food.

Chapter 8

Gabby

I toss the crust from the last piece of pizza into the box with disgust.

"I shouldn't have eaten all of that," I tell Chester my cat who watches me with interest from the coffee table. He takes the words as an invitation and leaps gracefully onto my lap. "Ugh," I moan as he steps on my full belly. "You've been eating too much, too."

Chester ignores the slight and curls onto me for a nap. I wrap my favorite yellow blanket around us and join him. I'm far from hungry now, but I'm still exhausted from the emotional morning.

My nap is interrupted by the chirping of my phone a few hours later. It takes a moment for me to remember why I'm on the couch. I rub my face hard with the heel of my hand, dig into my blurry eyes.

My phone stops ringing.

I push the empty pizza box to the side and find my phone under it. Darkness has fallen outside my windows and the time on my phone says just after six. This time of year in Indiana, it could either be six p.m. or six a.m. and still be dark out. Squinting at the phone, I see the tiny p.m. after the number. At least I didn't sleep around the clock.

The phone chirps in my hand, telling me the caller left a voicemail. I don't recognize the number and frankly don't care at the moment.

I toss the phone back on the coffee table and gather up the pizza box. "Better hide the evidence," I tell Chester.

After shoving the empty box to the bottom of my trash can, I sip a glass of water from the faucet and shake myself awake. Maybe finding Crystal and my fight with Lucas was just a dream? I splash cold water on my face and dry it with a dingy towel hanging on the stove door. The headache behind my scar still throbs, flashes of memory from this morning pounding through my head along with the pain. It wasn't a dream.

I toss the dirty towel across the kitchen in frustration and shame.

Crystal is dead.

I'd hurt Lucas.

Needing a release, I stalk across the floor and snatch the towel up. The rest of the evening passes in a blur of cleaning. I can't control the world, but I can control my small space. I'd rather go for a run, but the cold and dark keeps me locked in the house.

Chester hides behind the couch as I frantically scrub the counters and sweep the floors. Only when I fall into bed, tired but spent, does he come out of hiding. I wrap myself around my best friend.

The overcast morning sky does nothing to brighten my mood as I sip my coffee and stare out the front window of my house. Next door, I hear Preston start his car and leave for work. I freeze, hoping he doesn't see me at the window. We've barely spoken since that night in the woods at Halloween. The pain of his rejection has faded, added to the long list of similar reactions I've received from those I thought cared for me. Living next door to my ex-whatever-he-was has been awkward, but we've managed.

Once the sound of his car fades away, I drop the curtain back in place.

My house is spotless after last night's cleaning frenzy. The pristine conditions make me anxious. My rescheduled appointment with Ashley is a few hours away and I struggle to find something, anything, to keep my mind off of Crystal and Lucas.

The voicemail from last night offers a welcome distraction.

I barely recognize the voice on the message as Lucy Reed. The quiet mouse of a woman has transformed with her excitement.

"Gabby, this is Lucy Reed. I need to talk to you about what happened today. Please call me when you can." Simple and to the point, but the words tumble out of her at a pace I didn't think was possible.

The animation is still in her when I call back.

"Thank heavens you called," she gushes.

"What can I do for you?" I ask politely.

"Can you come see me this morning? I hate to ask, but I need to talk to someone."

Her unusual excitement sets my nerves on edge.

"I'll pay you the usual rate," she adds before giving me a chance to answer.

"I...." My eyes settle on my nearly-empty fridge. Since getting fired from my previous job and the costs of setting up my new shop, money has been tight. Guiltily, I agree, although talking about yesterday is at the bottom of my list of fun things to do to pass the time.

"You're a lifesaver," Lucy says. "I can't thank you enough."

Her dramatic response doesn't sit well. I almost prefer the silent, morose attitude she had before.

"Can you be here in an hour?" she continues.

"Sure. Where's here?" I dig a pen and pad out of the junk drawer, ready for an address.

"Bethel Stables," she says as if I should already have known.

I drop the pen on the counter.

"You know where it is?" she asks.

My mind scrambles to connect the massive property with the understated woman I met yesterday. "Of course I do. Everyone does. You own Bethel Stables?"

"Yes," she says simply, then hurries on, "Great, see you in an hour."

A moment of silence stretches.

"Thank you, Gabby. Really," Lucy says quietly, a small waver in her voice.

She hangs up before my mind can form a response.

I have no trouble finding Bethel Stables. It's a favorite place to drive by on my long, lonely explorations of the country roads surrounding River Bend. A classic wrought iron fence flanks the road approaching the property. Brick pillars stand as sentinels every so often, adding a touch of elegance. Behind the fence, several horses graze in the expansive pastures, nosing through the snow for hidden grasses. A few curious horses raise their heads as I turn past the beautiful Bethel Stables sign flanked by two statues of horses.

The asphalt has been plowed free of yesterday's snow and winds like a black snake through the pastures and up a hill. At the top of the hill, I park near a white colonial-style mansion. A bright green roof stands out against the white of the house and the white of the fields.

My old Charger looks out of place. The entire property screams money in an understated manner.

My footsteps echo across the silent snow as I walk past the white pillars that hold up a second-story wrap-around balcony. I lift the heavy brass door knocker with my gloved hand and drop it on the elaborate door. Above my head, a chandelier rocks gently in the winter breeze.

"This is Lucy Reed's?" I ask the swinging light. I search my mind for memories of Lucy. I vaguely remember her from high school as shy and intelligent. Nothing in my memories helps reconcile this glorious property with the woman. She still goes by her maiden name, so marrying into money doesn't make sense either. Apparently, Lucy's done very well for herself.

I suddenly wish I'd dressed nicer for this visit. My worn hiking boots and jeans don't seem to be the correct attire.

I shuffle nervously as the door remains unanswered. I drop the heavy knocker again and the noise carries across the quiet of the snow-covered pastures, reverberates through the house.

"Lucy?" I call to the house, "It's Gabby."

I step back from the door and look up to the balcony, searching for movement. The house is silent.

To the right of the property stands the stables and a large outdoor arena. The green roof and white walls match the house.

"Boarding a horse here probably costs more than my mortgage," I mutter as I cross to the stables looking for Lucy. Any guilt over charging her for this visit vanishes and is replaced with irritation. "Lucy?" I call out again as I push open the door to the stables. "You asked me to come, remember?"

The immensity of the barn overwhelms me. Four walkways branch off of a central indoor arena, each walkway flanked by stalls.

I listen for a response. The few horses that remain in their stalls instead of being turned out to pasture for the day nicker as I call for Lucy again.

A blur of black rushes out of the nearest stall-flanked walkway. I jump back and let out a startled shout. The black lab jumps against my legs in greeting, making me feel foolish for my fear.

"Hey boy," I rub behind the dog's ears, "Where's your

74

momma?"

The dog leans against my leg, then jumps again, unable to settle. He spins around, then rubs against me again, a whine deep in his throat.

My blood begins to sing with adrenaline as I realize my tattoo is tingling. I take two steps into the stables and look cautiously down the walkway. The far end is blocked by a gate, but the walkway is empty.

I call to Lucy again, and the dog whines.

A stall door clatters and a horse snorts angrily, causing my already taut nerves to jump. I duck under a board blocking the walkway from the rest of the barn and take a few cautious steps towards the agitated horse. The chalkboard plaque says Razor.

The spotted horse snorts at me and kicks at the stall door.

"Shh," I soothe, not at all sure how to talk to a horse. "Everything's okay."

Razor raises on his back legs and paws at the bars on the top half of his stall in response.

The dog whines.

"Shh," I say to them both, as well as myself.

Razor pushes his nose against the bars and I reach to pet the soft skin. He pulls away and circles the small, blowing air.

Beneath his feet, I see the toe of a rubber boot.

I cling to the bars to pull myself higher above the wood wall so I can see better. I can only see the other boot and the beginnings of jean-clad legs.

Razor kicks again and I let go of the bars. Covered

with heavy winter gloves, my shaking fingers fumble on the sliding latch of the stall door. Sensing my growing panic, Razor circles the stall again, blowing and snorting.

I manage to slide the heavy door open.

Razor bolts into the walkway, knocking me to the dirt. His heavy hooves pound the ground as he runs past. He reaches the gate at the end of the walkway, rears up, then rushes towards me.

The dog runs out, away from the wild horse.

I push to my feet and flatten my body against the door of an empty stall. Trapped in the walkway, Razor runs back and forth, his hooves dangerously close to my feet.

With my back to the wall, I slide towards the gate that leads outside, murmuring what I hope are calming sounds to the horse.

Once at the gate, I wait until Razor is at the far end of the walkway, then open the latch as quickly as possible.

Sensing freedom, the horse bolts at a full gallop. He brushes past me and takes off across the snow.

I slam the gate closed, checking to make sure it latches, then rush to the body in the stall.

Chapter 9

Gabby

The black lab beats me into the stall. He nuzzles at the badly broken body. His whine tears at my heart.

I drop onto my knees, unsure of what to do.

From the huge permed hair, I know instantly it's Lucy. One arm and both of her legs jut at odd angles. Bloody hoof prints show where Razor had stepped and pawed at her, killing her.

Lucy lies perfectly still, like a broken doll tossed on the ground.

Her skin has turned white beneath the blood on her face. Her eyes stare sightlessly past me at the wall.

Yesterday's grief over finding Crystal combines with grief over this woman I barely knew. I pull her lifeless body into my arms and bury my face into her coat.

"I'm so sorry," I sob to them both. "I'm so sorry."

Sitting on my knees amidst the sawdust and manure, I cradle Lucy. Rocking with the ache of sorrow torn from deep within me, I shake with heaving sobs. My nose fills and I raise my head to wipe it.

Lucy's blood stains my glove. I stare at the stain, then look to the ceiling.

"Why did you take her?" I scream to God, not sure if I mean Lucy or Crystal. "Why did you do this?"

A soft nicker from another part of the stables is God's only response.

From my lap, Lucy's lifeless eyes stare up at me, snapping me back to the present. As gently as possible, I slide her body off and climb to my feet. My legs wobble so badly, I cling to the bars on the stalls to get out of the stables.

The dog remains with Lucy.

I need air.

The door leading to outside won't open. I panic, kicking and heaving my shoulder into the panel. I try the handle again and the door swings open suddenly. I crash onto the sidewalk and gulp the fresh air. Blood covers my gloves and coat. I crawl to a pile of shoveled snow, scoop up handfuls and scrub. The snow turns pink and falls to the ground.

Blood still stains my gloves. I pull them off and throw them. A breeze catches them and blows them back to me.

"Get away!" I scream at the gloves and throw them again. They land on the pristine snow, dark red stains against the white.

The symbol of my gifts stained with Lucy's innocent blood sears my soul.

"I don't want this!" I scream at God. "I can't do what you need me to. There's too much death, too much pain."

The property of Bethel Stables surrounds me in gray winter silence.

"Do you hear me? I can't do this anymore."

I wrap my arms around my knees and lay my head on the pile of snow. "Please," I beg. "I'm not strong enough."

A cloud breaks overhead. The sunlight suddenly reflected on the snow burns my eyes.

My tattoo sizzles.

Get up.

"I don't want to," I reply. "I don't want to do any of it."

An electric shock runs up my arm, so strong I jump in pain.

The sunlight glitters against my squinting eyes.

Get up and get to work.

The pain in my arm increases, grows unbearable. I rub the spot angrily, but it won't stop.

I finally obey and climb to my feet.

The shock from my tattoo subsides.

I take out my phone to call for help.

The pain from my tattoo disappears.

My finger hovers over Lucas' name in my contacts. I need him, I want him here. But he won't want to talk to me.

I scroll up to Dustin's number, but can't bring myself to push the icon.

I turn my face to the bright slash of sunshine pouring through the break in the clouds. The light glows behind my closed eyelids. The warmth of the sun caresses my cheeks. A peace soaks into me, the feeling out of place with Lucy lying trampled to death nearby.

I scroll back to Lucas's number and push the icon, hoping for the best.

"I'm really not ready to talk to you," Lucas says instead of hello.

"I understand," I say, secretly thrilled just to hear his voice. "But we have a problem."

"You think?" he snarks. "What, did I kill someone else?"

The sharp words make my breath catch in my throat. "Maybe this was a bad idea," I stall. "Is Dustin there?"

"Man, what did you do to tick him off?" Dustin asks on the line.

"This isn't the time to get into it," I reply. "Look, I'm out at Bethel Stables. Lucy Reed wanted to talk to me this morning."

Even through the phone, I can sense Dustin's mood changing. "Something bad happened, didn't it?" I hear the unspoken comment loud and clear. *Something bad happens wherever you go.*

"She was trampled to death by one of her horses," I say in a rush.

"Is there anyone else there with you?" his tone is all cop now.

"I haven't seen anyone." I scan the property, but my Charger is the only car.

Dustin covers the phone and says something to Lucas. "We'll be right there. Don't touch anything."

I don't have the heart to tell him I already touched plenty. He'll be disappointed enough when he gets here.

My rear grows cold as I sit on a bench near the stalls waiting for them. I shift uncomfortably and pull my coat tighter. I could have waited in my car where it was warmer, but I wanted to stay near Lucy. The black dog waits nearby.

The slam of a car door alerts me to their arrival. No lights and sirens this time. Lucy is beyond help.

I open the door that leads outside, this time remembering to turn the handle all the way to get it to open. Lucas hangs a few steps behind Dustin, but my eyes search him out immediately. His head is turned away from me, seemingly more interested in the horses in the pasture than me finding yet another dead body.

I raise my chin, ignoring the slight. "She's over here," I say to Dustin, stepping away from the door to let them enter. "Fourth stall on the right."

I retake my seat on the bench, pretend not to care that Lucas still hasn't acknowledged my existence. I rub the dog's head, his fur warming my bare hands.

After examining the scene, Dustin comes to me, notebook open and ready. "Start from the beginning," he sighs, watching Lucas go back outside. He raises questioning eyebrows at Lucas' departure, but doesn't ask any questions. If Lucas hasn't told him anything, I won't either.

Instead, I explain the events of the morning.

"The horse is out in the pasture now?" Dustin asks, glancing down the walkway to the gate at the far end.

"I guess," I say. "Wherever that gate leads to."

Dustin studies me, nodding at the stains on the front of my coat. "Want to explain how her blood got on you?"

I look down at my coat. "Not really." My handling of Lucy and crying all over her was not one of my best moments. The poor woman deserved better.

"I suppose that's all." He snaps his notebook closed. "You didn't get any, you know, from her?"

I shake my head. "Actually, I got nothing. I was wearing heavy gloves, though." We both look at my bare hands. My mouth goes dry and I swallow hard. "Do you want me to…?"

Lucas opens the door suddenly. "I called the coroner," he says to Dustin, then shuts the door again without looking at me.

I feel like I've been slapped. "Can I go now?"

Dustin moves his feet uncomfortably. "That's fine," he says in his cop voice. "Are you going to Grandma's?" he asks in his brother voice.

Lucas' dismissal still rankles and I take it out on Dustin. "I don't need to go running to Grandma and have her kiss it all better," I snap.

The kind expression he briefly wore disappears.

Instantly contrite, I mutter, "I'm sorry. It's been a rough couple days."

Dustin wears his blank cop face now. "I'm sure it has."

"Besides, I have an appointment in a little while," I say lamely.

"We'll be in touch," he says. "Looks like an accident, so we shouldn't need you for anything."

Shouldn't need me for anything.

I tuck the sting away with the hundreds of other stings I've collected.

At least Ashley needs me to do a reading for her. I cling to that tiny satisfaction as I leave Bethel Stables. The horses in the pasture raise their heads as I drive by, oblivious to the drama in the barn. At a far corner of the pasture, I see Razor nosing for grass. In the snow around him, tiny smears of blood rub from his hooves.

Chapter 10

Lucas

"You look like crap," Dustin says as he takes his seat at his desk that faces mine.

I rub my face, wishing I had shaved this morning. "Rough night," I say simply.

Dustin eyes the collection of empty coffee cups on my desk. "Looks like a rough morning, too."

Rough doesn't begin to describe it. The few fitful hours of sleep I managed to get were plagued with nightmares of Crystal calling out for me as she died. Confusing images of Gabby swirled through the dreams, too. Stirring feelings I wasn't willing to analyze once I woke up.

I look at my silent cell phone sitting next to the empty cups for the hundredth time since my fight with Gabby yesterday. I want it to ring, want her to call begging for forgiveness.

As if summoned by my mind, her name appears on the incoming call screen.

Nervous fear shoots through me. *I'm not ready. I'm not*

ready.

I tell her as much when I answer. Hating myself for the pain I hear in her voice.

On the drive to Bethel Stables, Dustin has the good sense to keep his mouth shut about his sister. I silently thank him for not pushing, while my belly rolls with nerves.

I don't want to see her.

When she opens the door, her face streaked with blood, I almost give in. She's obviously been crying and a deep need to comfort her washes through me.

I scan the property instead.

Processing Lucy's accident doesn't take long. I struggle to keep my mind on the job, on the dead woman who deserves my full attention.

I'm acutely aware Gabby waits on a bench just a few yards away.

I'm acutely aware I shouldn't care. She thought I killed my sister.

As soon as professionally possible, I escape into the fresh air. Dustin can take her statement. Dustin can answer the questions. Dustin can hold her if she needs it.

I kick at a pile of snow outside the door, hating myself for my cowardice. I should be holding her. I should be asking the questions. I should forgive her.

I'm not ready. I'm not ready.

Pink stains of blood-smeared snow surround the pile I kick at. Looking closer, I see the imprint of knee marks on the ground. It's easy to see where Gabby must have kneeled and scrubbed blood off of her. A yard or so away, her bloody gloves lay forgotten.

The discarded gloves sting my heart. Gabby's gloves are her protection from the world. They're symbols of her gift. She must have been very upset to throw them away and leave them here.

On impulse, I retrieve the blood-stained gloves from the snow and slide them into a plastic bag. They aren't evidence, but I don't want the blood to get on anything else. While I put the bagged gloves into the cruiser, Gabby's Charger roars to life.

I watch the gray car as it winds down the drive to the road.

Ready or not, she left.

"The coroner's on her way?" Dustin asks, suddenly behind my shoulder.

I pull my eyes from the now-empty driveway. "Yeah," I reply lamely.

"Normally, I'd say it's none of my business, and honestly I don't want to know. But what the hell?" Dustin nods to the road where Gabby's car just disappeared.

"It's complicated," I hedge.

"Everything with Gabby is complicated." Dustin leans on the hood of the cruiser. "We have time."

I rub my hand across my chilled face. "She found Crystal yesterday."

"I know that already. I was there."

I struggle for the correct words. "When she, saw, what she saw, she said Crystal was saying my name."

Dustin crosses his arms over his chest and waits for me to continue.

"She thought I killed her," I blurt.

Dustin stares intently at the overcast sky. "I figured as much when she called me and not you, then refused to tell you about it."

A long moment of silence stretches between us.

"But she did tell you. And you said 'thought.' Past-tense. She came to her senses pretty quickly."

"Not quickly enough," I grumble. "How could she think I had anything to do with what happened to Crystal?" My voice raises embarrassingly.

Dustin shrugs, his practiced nonchalance annoying. "We both know that those closest to the victim are often the perpetrators. I'm the last person to defend Gabby and her craziness, but if she really did find Crystal and really did see your name in Crystal's mind, it was a logical conclusion to come to."

I huff, not wanting to see the logic.

"Look, you two do what you want, but we both know Gabby works on a level different than normal people. If you want to be friends with my sister, you better buckle up or get off the ride."

A reluctant chuckle pulls from my throat. "Never a dull moment," I motion to our current location.

"Exactly." Dustin uncrosses his arms and straightens to his full height. "I have no choice about being involved with her. You, at least, have the option of choosing."

I kick snow off my boots, growing uncomfortable with the emotional conversation. "Do you think Crystal was murdered?" I ask suddenly, surprising us both.

Dustin shrugs again. "She saw something in that

cemetery."

I kick the last minuscule spot of snow from my boot. "I need to know for sure," I say to the ground. "My parents need to know for sure. They're pretty shook up over this."

"It will take a court order," Dustin replies, following my train of thought. "Annette Reed already gave verbal permission to exhume her dad's grave." Dustin darts his eyes to the stables. "Of course, losing her daughter might change her mind."

"Or solidify it," I point out. "A bit of a coincidence Lucy would be trampled to death after what happened yesterday."

"My thoughts, exactly." The approaching black van draws our attention. "Let's see what the coroner has to say first."

"And one of us has to talk to Annette Reed." My stomach sinks with the gravity of the situation. "I'll do it," I offer. Delivering death notices to family is the hardest part of this job. Dustin is a great detective, but I'm better with the emotional parts.

"You're a good man, Hartley. Take the cruiser. I'll catch a ride back with the coroner's team."

I push all thoughts of Gabby and of Crystal out of my mind as I drive. Annette Reed just lost her only daughter. She deserves my full attention.

Chapter 11

Gabby

The water from the faucet in the small bathroom attached to the upstairs apartment at my shop refuses to get warm enough. Scooping handfuls of cool water, I scrub blood off my face. Pink tinged water runs across the cracked porcelain and dribbles down the drain. I rub until my face hurts, but still feel stained by Lucy's death.

The door downstairs jingles as the water turns to clear. "Be right there," I holler to Ashley, then slide a pair of clean gloves over my damp hands.

Ashley clings to the same plastic bag she brought with her yesterday. She hovers near the front door but offers me a shaky smile as I descend the stairs.

I force a professional tone and ignore the residual quaking in my knees. "Come on in. Have a seat." I motion to the couch and chairs I've set up to meet with clients.

Ashley takes the seat closest to the door, her bottom perched on the edge of the cushion.

"Thanks for rescheduling." She sets the plastic bag next to her on the couch as I take my place on a facing chair.

"Sorry about yesterday," I say sincerely. "Today's not been much better, but I didn't want to put you off again."

Ashley's pinched face relaxes into concern. "Everything okay?"

Her earnest worry breaks my professional façade. "Not really." I shoot a quick glance at the door, half expecting Lacey to return digging for more details about Lucy. "Lucy Reed was killed by one of her horses this morning."

Ashley gasps in surprise. "Little Lucy Reed? How awful." Ashley studies my face. "Did you find her?"

"I did. How did you…."

"You have blood," Ashley touches the side of her face. I scrub at my temple with my fresh glove.

"Crap on a cracker." I swallow hard to keep my voice from breaking. "Did I get it?"

"All good," Ashley says gently.

I fix my eyes on the brick wall behind her for a moment, getting myself together, then ask, "What can I do for you?"

Ashley slides the plastic bag onto the coffee table between us. "I have a problem. Or at least I think I do. Seems kind of stupid now, with Crystal and now Lucy dead." It's her turn to stare behind me, thinking. "They were friends in high school, you know."

I don't pretend to know who hung out with who back then. I only remember sitting alone.

"They were?"

"Lucy and I had chemistry class together. She was

always such a mouse, you know. Wanted so badly to belong. You know the type."

I nod. I was that type.

"She eventually fell into Crystal's group. I only remember because Lucy seemed too sweet to be part of that crowd."

I politely don't point out that Ashley hung out with Lacey and her popular cronies. As far as I ever saw, no one in Lacey's group was sweet.

"Who else did she hang out with back then?" I ask, intrigued by the lesson of what should have been my own history.

Ashley stares at the wall behind me again. "Let's see, Crystal, Lucy, Vee, Lane a few others. Bunch of stoners, you know?"

"Vee and Lane? The couple that own the Kingston Winery? They just catered my grand opening party."

"Huh, small world, but yes, them. They weren't what I'd call over-achievers. Mostly hung out at that old shack on the river behind Crystal's house. Lacey and I went there once." Ashley continues, getting into the flow of her nostalgia. "It was definitely not my scene. Mostly drinking, smoking pot, fooling around, that type of thing."

She looks at me as if that was a normal part of my high school days. "Of course," I say lamely.

"Guess you can't judge a person by what they were like in high school. Vee and Lane own the winery now and Lucy has that huge horse stables. They all did pretty well for themselves." Ashley's voice catches and she slides the bag closer to me. "And I'm here needing you to tell me if my husband is having an affair."

The quick switch back to the present takes a moment to process. "An affair?"

"This is one of his shirts. He's been acting off lately, you know. Like coming home later than he used to, that type of thing. I didn't know who to turn to. I don't want to confront him unless I have proof."

She stares miserably at the bag holding her husband's shirt. I don't really need to touch it. If she's this upset, she's probably right. Female intuition is pretty powerful.

"You want me to touch the shirt and tell you what I see? I might not get something from it. And if I do, are you sure you want to know?"

Her head slips lower as the gravity of the situation sinks into her.

I hate to do this to her, Ashley deserves better than a cheating husband. "Before I do it, there's the small matter of my payment." My cheeks burn with embarrassment. I'm not sure I'll ever get used to this part.

"Oh, of course." Ashley pays me, then waits expectantly. "Will you be able to tell who it is?"

"I don't know. Do you have someone in mind you think he's with?"

She turns her head away, a sure sign she does.

I pull the bag onto my lap, then slide off my left glove. "Lord, let me see what I need to see," I pray silently.

I clutch the fabric in my bare fingers, and it only takes a moment to get the answer.

"I'm sorry, Ashley, I really am."

She keeps her head turned away from me, wipes at a

tear sliding down her cheek. "Is she blond?"

"I didn't see a blond. Dark hair, I think."

Her shoulders sink with relief. "Not a blond. Thank God." She stands suddenly and snaps the bag away from me. "Thank you for your help, Gabby. Really, thank you."

"You're welcome," I say, not sure I helped her at all.

"This meeting is confidential, right? You won't tell anyone about it?" She stands near the chair I sit in, her agitation making me uncomfortable.

"Of course," I stand pointedly, and she's forced to take a step back. "You can trust me to be discreet."

"Perfect." She turns towards the door, the plastic bag swinging in an arc around her.

The door slams as she leaves in a huff, a different woman than when she came in.

Staring at the small, gothic style courthouse on the square across the street from my shop, I mull over what Ashley said about Lucy and Crystal and the group of friends that used to hang out at the shack on the river. Not long after Crystal and I drifted apart, her family moved from the modest houses in our neighborhood to a much larger property south of town. It's another property I've admired on my lonely country drives. I'd heard from Grandma Dot that Lucas' mother, Deidre, had designed the expansive house. As I recall, Grandma said Deidre had driven the builder crazy with last-minute changes and exacting details. "Should have just bought an old farmhouse like this," Grandma had said. "And leave that poor builder alone."

With my sullen attitude towards Crystal at the time, I'd

relished every bit of gossip about Deidre's antics and secretly hoped she was driving Crystal nuts as well. If I'd known Crystal only had a few short time left to live, I'd have been more sympathetic.

A scrap of paper blows down the sidewalk across the street. Its forlorn dance unsettles me, as it skitters and swirls alone. I turn my back to the window and busy myself with paperwork and setting appointments for a few new clients. At least the opening party wasn't a total disaster, my e-mail has more messages than normal. Once again, Grandma Dot was right.

The busy work only occupies me for so long and the quiet of the shop makes me itchy.

I suddenly slam the laptop shut. "Who are you kidding?" I ask the empty space. "You know you're going to drive out there."

Lucy's blood on the front of my coat makes me wince. The stains nearly blend in with the dark blue fabric now that they've dried. If I do this right, I won't see anyone, so the stains won't matter.

When the beautiful house that Deidre Hartley built comes into view, uncertainty niggles at my brain. I can't just walk up to the house and ask if I can explore their riverbank. I drive past the property and pull over near the bridge down the road. One front wheel of my Charger slides off the side of the road, but the other three tires hold. I might have trouble getting out of the snow when I leave, but decide to worry about that later.

The slam of my door echoes loudly across the empty river. Broken sheets of ice reach like gnarled fingers from the banks into the black water flowing timelessly at the river's center. The eternal movement of the water draws my eyes hypnotically.

I shake my head to focus on my mission and trudge into the woods lining the banks.

It only takes a few minutes for the isolation of the woods to engulf me. My car waits a hundred yards or so behind and the Hartley house is not far away to my right, but trekking through the quiet woods, I might as well be a thousand miles from nowhere.

Snow slips down into my hiking boots and my toes soon ache with cold. Feeling foolish, I realize that the shack was probably torn down years ago. The rest of the Hartley property is pristine, small chance they'd leave a run-down eyesore out here for so long. I should have checked with someone that the shack was still here. But who could I call?

I stop on a hill and scan the woods, torn between turning back and pressing further into the trees.

I listen to the wind, listen to my tattoo.

The river's quiet gurgle is the only response.

"I give up," I mutter.

Turning to retrace my steps, my boot slips on a patch of ice hidden below snowy leaves. Facedown on the hill, I slide, my knee colliding with a fallen branch painfully. At the bottom of the hill, I roll onto my rear.

Cold seeps into the seat of my jeans as I rub at my sore knee. "Crap on a cracker, that hurt."

I straighten and bend my leg a few times, testing my knee. "Just rub some dirt on it," I mutter and climb to my feet.

My knee holds my weight and after a few steps, the pain subsides.

Just bruised, could have been worse.

And no one knows I'm out here.

The thought sobers me instantly. Trespassing alone in the frozen woods when no one knows I'm here is definitely not one of my best ideas.

A few more ginger steps around the low area I fell into, and I'm sure my knee is fine. Behind me, a branch breaks in the woods and I spin at the sound.

Dark tree trunks surround me. A squirrel chatters in the distance.

But nothing jumps out of the woods to tackle me.

Squinting up the next hill, an unnaturally straight piece of wood catches my attention. Patches of peeling white paint on the weathered wood blend into the trees and snow, but the straight lines give it away.

I found the shack.

Chapter 12

Gabby

My hurt knee forgotten, I scramble up the hill to the shack. Whatever the slant-roof building's original use was is lost to time and decay. The whole thing leans to the right at a dangerous angle, looking like one more harsh winter storm would bring it to the ground. The original white paint has peeled off in large chunks. Graffiti mars the paint still clinging to the wood.

A large blue heart dominates the wall next to the front door. The words "Lucas Loves Ka..." with the rest of her name missing stuns me. It's hard to picture the straight-laced Lucas I know now as a lovesick teen spray-painting his name in a heart with a mysterious girl. I wrack my brain for a Kay, Katelyn, Kayla, Kara, any girl from school Lucas thought he loved.

No one jumps to mind. The heart and names stir a jealous surge I have no right to feel. I touch the faded paint and peel a chip away. More chips fall to the frozen ground, and the Ka is gone.

Feeling both satisfied and petty, I push on the battered

door hanging by one hinge.

It takes several shoves until the door swings into the dark interior of the shack. The heavy scent of animal waste and rotting wood assails my nose. I peer inside, braced for a raccoon or rats or something sinister to fly at me.

Nothing worse than the nasty smell attacks me, so I step inside.

The dirt floor is uneven, shifted by years of freezing and thaw. Light seeps through widening gaps in the wood planks of the walls. A portion of the roof in a far corner has caved in.

Even as a hang-out for teens wanting to smoke and party, it's nasty. I'd been a little envious when Ashley told me all the kids had come here for fun and I was never invited. Even accounting for years of neglect, I can't imagine this place as one I'd want to spend time in.

Some rusted metal folding chairs lean against one wall. A few plastic lawn chairs lean on broken legs. A folding table sags below a window, covered with a thick coat of dust and chewed nutshells from squirrel activity. Empty beer cans and plastic cups litter the table, as well as glass bottles that once held liquor. My original intention had been to touch things here, hope for a vision of anything that would point to Crystal's killer. Everything is so filthy, I can't bring myself to pull off my gloves, let alone touch something.

A bare mattress, torn to shreds by mice, lies in a lumpy mess in another corner. No way I'm touching it. Even if it was clean, I have no interest in visions of groping teens doing who knows what to each other on it.

Piles of dirt and gravel surround the mattress. On closer inspection, dark tunnels lead from the piles under the mattress. I recognize the piles and tunnels from similar ones Grandma Dot deals with on her farm. Groundhogs are horribly destructive and hard to get rid of.

I kick loose gravel down a tunnel, "Nasty varmints," I mutter at the dark hole.

My kicking loosens something shiny. Even in the faded light inside the shack, I recognize the coin as gold.

The glittering circle nearly glows against the dingy backdrop of the shack. I pick it up and turn it over in my gloved palm.

The coin has a cross stamped on one side and a coat of arms on the other.

I gasp in excitement at the find. I'm no historian, but it looks like a gold Spanish doubloon. I exit the shack, eager to see the coin in the light.

"Has to be a fake," I say out loud, pulling my left glove off, anxious to touch the gold.

"Maverick!" a man's shout tears through the woods, making me jump.

The gold coin tumbles from my palm and into the snow.

Startled, I shove through the snow until my fingers wrap around the coin.

A massive white dog, covered in black spots bounds out of the trees, his long tongue flopping out of his mouth.

I shove the coin in my pocket and turn my attention to

the Great Dane. Luckily, he's more interested in licking my face than attacking me.

"Mav? Where are you?" The man's shouts for his dog are closer this time.

I freeze in indecision. Should I hide? Fat chance, the dog will give me away. I shove the spotted Great Dane away, irritated.

The man appears, leaving me no choice but to confess my presence.

He stops short when he sees me. Even with longer hair and a full beard, the man's resemblance to Lucas is instantly apparent.

"Hi, Mr. Hartley," I say with an awkward wave, trying to keep the huge dog from jumping on me at the same time.

Curiously, Mr. Hartley doesn't seem that surprised to see me. "Looks like we had the same idea today, Gabby," he says. With the gold coin heavy in my pocket, it takes me a moment to follow his train of thought. "Crystal loved coming here," he continues wistfully. "You probably have lots of memories of here."

I don't have the heart to tell him this is my first time coming to the shack.

"I'm so sorry about what happened with Crystal," I say honestly. "It was quite a shock." I push on the dog again.

"Maverick, down," Mr. Hartley commands. Maverick lies at my feet, his huge head on his paws. "Must have been hardest on you," he adds. "Finding her like that."

I focus on Maverick so I don't have to meet his eyes. "It wasn't pleasant." I finger the coin in my pocket debating whether or not to tell him what I found. "I'm sorry I trespassed, Mr. Hartley," I say to stall.

His blue eyes, so like Lucas', search mine. "Call me Gregor. We're practically family."

His easy manner is so soothing, I understand how he became such a prominent psychiatrist. "Family?"

"You were so close to Crystal as kids. And now you and Lucas are...." He trails off, waiting for me to fill in the blank.

"Not talking at the moment," I offer, pulling my empty hand out of my pocket.

If the admission shocked him, he doesn't show it. Instead, he looks pointedly at the freshly peeled wood of the heart, then at me. "Only a passing squabble. Lucas cares for you. He talks about you all the time."

My cheeks burn against the cold air. "Most people talk about me," I point out. "Few people like me."

Gregor laughs at this. "That's how you know you're doing the right things. You can't make it far in this world without ruffling a few feathers." His face turns solemn. "Crystal was good at ruffling feathers."

"I hate to ask this, but do you have any idea who would want to hurt her?"

"All these years, I thought she'd just run away. She was always fighting with Deidre, and even squabbling with Lucas. Just normal teen stuff. I figured she'd outgrow it. Rebellion is a necessary phase of development."

He looks to me, seemingly waiting for an answer. I shrug in response.

"When she ran away, I was sure she'd run wild for a

103

while, then come back. When she never contacted us again, it hurt. Really hurt."

A shrug doesn't seem appropriate, so I say, "I can imagine."

"On the one hand, it's easier knowing she couldn't contact us, not that she didn't want to see us ever again. Does that make sense?" He doesn't wait for a response. "Knowing my baby girl was murdered years ago is such a shock. I don't know how to process the change to my belief system about the situation."

"Being able to lay her to rest properly and say good-bye is a good place to start."

Gregor looks at the shack, mulls over my suggestion. "You're sure she's there? That she's in someone else's grave?" he asks without looking at me.

"I can't ever be completely sure about the things I see," I hedge.

"But you did see her? You saw her murder?"

"In a way."

"But you don't know who did it? With all your abilities, you don't know that simple fact?" His voice rises and two spots of red appear above his beard.

I sigh heavily. "Trust me. More than anyone else, I wish I could see more. I never pretend to be able to control it."

"Of course, of course." The red spots fade. "I'm sorry I snapped."

If that was the extent of his snapping, I could teach him a thing or two. "No apologies necessary. This is hard on all of us, not knowing for sure," I prod again.

Gregor continues to stare at the shack. "I have a judge friend who owes me a favor," he mutters. "I think I'll place a call." He snaps his fingers at Maverick and the dog jumps to his long legs.

"You won't tell Lucas I was here, will you?" The question pops out of my mouth before I can take it back.

Gregor turns his full smile on me. "Your secret's safe with me, Gabby. But don't let this little squabble go on too long. You'll never find a better man than my son, but he can be stubborn. Something tells me stubbornness is a trait you're very familiar with."

"Maybe." I smile shyly. "You're a sweet man, Gregor. I see where Lucas gets it from."

"Tell you what. On Friday, Deidre is hosting a fundraiser at the antique car museum over in Coburn. Lucas is required by his mother to attend every year. He'll need a date."

"Lucas can find his own dates."

"He doesn't want to find a different one. You make up with him before Friday. I'm counting on seeing you at that party." Gregor winks at me, then calls to Maverick. They disappear into the trees before I can refuse.

I stand alone outside of the shack, my mouth hanging open in surprise.

Chapter 13

GABBY

Gregor's words about stubbornness echo through my mind as I make the long trek back to my car. My pride still stings from Lucas ignoring me this morning, but pride and stubbornness have no place in a relationship.

Either does sneaking around on his parents' property.

Once in my car, the heater running, I call Lucas, mentally crossing my fingers that he'll answer.

"Hi," he warily answers on the fourth ring.

"Hey," I say awkwardly, my mouth suddenly dry, my mind at a loss for words.

The line remains silent for a few tense beats. "It's been a long day, Gabby," he says with an edge to his voice.

"I know, I'm sorry." I rub my hand across the worn leather of my steering wheel. "Can we talk? I'd really like to talk to you."

He sighs heavily. "I just left Annette Reed's and I'm headed out to see my parents now. Can we meet later?"

"I, um, I'm actually just down the road from your parents right now."

He blows air in exasperation. "Why are you at my parents'? Never mind, I don't want to know."

"I want you to know. That's part of why I called." He hasn't hung up on me yet. I take that as a good sign and push my advantage. "I'm parked by the bridge. Can you meet me here?"

On the far side of the bridge, I see his car approaching. "I'm already there."

He hangs up and I wonder if he'll just drive past me.

He parks on the other side of the road.

My belly swims and my arms feel weak with nervous energy now that he's here. I thought I'd have more time to prepare.

I shut the door of the Charger and lean against the car. He leans against his cruiser on the opposite side of the road, the strip of slushy asphalt between us. His face looks crumpled and tired and I have a sudden urge to run my hand down his cheek and smooth the hurt away.

"Can we walk?" I ask, motioning to the bridge. He pushes himself away from his car and takes a few steps in the direction of the bridge, his hand shoved deep into his pockets.

My feet move on the side of the road, but my tongue refuses to form words.

"What did you want to talk about?" Lucas grumbles from his side of the road.

Just be honest. Truly honest.

"You've always been a good friend to me, Lucas." Once the words start, they fall like snow. "You've been the one person I could always count on. No matter what I saw, or thought I saw, I shouldn't have doubted you. You've never doubted me."

"That's true," he says cautiously.

We've reached the center of the bridge and I stop walking, turn to face him. "Finding Crystal scared the crap out of me. Hearing your name in her mind scared me even more." I swipe at my nose that's begun to run and take a step across the road. "I know it's not an excuse, but I just want you to know where I was coming from." I hate the desperate tone of my voice, but owe it to him.

He takes a step towards me. "I always know where you're coming from. It's been my curse, always having your back."

I take another step towards him, search his face for forgiveness. "I know that being my friend isn't easy." I wipe at my nose again, angry that my eyes are watering too. "It's not exactly easy being me."

I step again, nearly reaching the yellow centerline.

I wait for his response, watch the emotions as they play over his so-familiar face. "I can only tell you I'm sorry." I continue, taking another step. I swallow hard and force myself to say the words that have been swirling in my head the last day. "I need you Lucas. Nothing else in my life is as important as our friendship. I need you."

Our eyes lock across the last few feet of the road between us. The world around me disappears. All that matters is his next words.

The blast of a horn shatters the moment. A car swerves behind me, annoyed we're blocking the narrow bridge road. A gust of wind from the car pushes me. and Lucas grabs the front of my coat pulling me away from the car.

The car honks angrily and drives away.

Lucas crushes me to his chest.

"Looks like I'm always saving you," he says, his face so close I clearly see the crinkles of humor at the corners of his blue eyes.

"I told you I need you." I lick my dry lips. His eyes watch the path my tongue takes.

"You're wrong, though," he nearly whispers. "I don't want to be your friend."

He still holds the front of my coat and uses it to pull me closer to his body. Even in the cold, I can feel the heat of his thighs against mine. The scant air between us crackles.

I take the plunge. "I don't want to be your friend either," I breathe.

Pushing up on the toes of my boots, I lift my mouth to his, half afraid he'll push me away.

His lips lower, hesitate a delicious moment.

I push higher on my toes. His mouth is warm and firm, and unbelievably right. I sink into the moment, the exquisite moment.

His hands release my coat and slide behind my shoulders. Our bodies crush together as our mouths explore.

When the kiss ends, I let him hold me, weak and breathless. Below us, the dark water continues its quiet, eternal journey. Through his coat and the protective vest of his uniform, I can hear his heartbeat against my ear, another eternal sound.

"Does this mean you forgive me?" I ask.

Lucas pushes me back so he can see my face. "You talk too much," he says, then kisses me again. A shiver runs through my body at the contact.

"Are you cold?"

"Not really. Just amazed." I burrow into his arms, hoping the moment will last forever.

The radio on his shoulder crackles. I jump in surprise and crash back to reality.

"Anything serious?" I ask.

"Nothing to worry about." He tips my chin up and drops a light peck on my lips. "I do need to get moving. I've got to talk to my parents, then head back to the station."

I cock my head in question.

"Annette Reed has agreed to allow us to…." His voice trails away. "I just need to discuss it with my parents first."

"Your dad wants to find out for sure, too. He said he had to make a call or something."

"My dad?"

"I ran into him down at the shack where Crystal and her friends used to hang out." I tuck my head on his chest so he can't see the burning of my cheeks. "I kind of trespassed this morning."

"So that's why you're out here. I'm sure there's a story there, but it will have to wait til later."

I release him reluctantly when he pulls away. Hugging the side of the road, we return to our parked cars. He takes my gloved hand in his as we walk. Even through the gloves, tingles run up my arm.

At my car, Lucas inspects the front tire that slid off the road into the snow. "Looks like you might be stuck," he chuckles.

"Good thing you came along," I quip back, bumping my shoulder into his.

"I'm glad I came," he says, suddenly serious.

"Me too," I breathe. The intensity of his look makes me shy and awkward. I let go of his hand and climb into the car, frightened by my reaction and the new feelings he's stirred up.

Gunning the gas, I try to back onto the road. My front tire throws snow into the air. Lucas pushes at the front bumper and the car jumps out of the rut.

I take off a glove and put my arm out the rolled-down window. He removes his own glove and our bare palms touch. The sizzle his skin sends into me has nothing to do with my psychic abilities. I squeeze his hand and meet his eyes. No words are required as he backs away to his cruiser.

In my side-view mirror, I watch him watch me drive away until the reflection is too small to make out.

A feeling of peace I've never known settles over me. I grin like a madwoman the whole drive home, happier than I've been in years.

Chapter 14

Dustin

Sweat drips down my chest as I walk up the steps to the kitchen from my basement gym. My arms ache pleasantly from my early morning work-out. I increased the weights this morning and I'm satisfied with my progress.

I lift the hem of my tank top and wipe the sweat off my face as I wait for a glass of water to fill from the tap. I gulp the water greedily then put the glass in the empty sink. It looks out of place in the kitchen Alexis cleaned before we went to bed.

A quick wash and a towel dry and I put the glass away in the cupboard. Alexis works so hard to keep our house clean, I don't need her to wake up to a dirty dish thoughtlessly left behind. The tiny act fills me with a different kind of satisfaction.

The coffee maker gurgles and drips in the quiet kitchen. Outside, the first faint glow of daybreak dances across the front yard, and my mind turns to the work ahead of me today.

The exhumation of Crystal Hartley.

Mostly what I remember of Crystal is the scrawny, annoying girl who tagged along with Gabby when we were kids. A few times, I'd let them play video games with me. Until their chatter and giggling got on my nerves and I'd send them away. She'd just been that friend of my sister's, not worth my notice or my time. At some point, she'd stopped coming over, and honestly, I'd never thought about her again.

Until later when Lucas and I became partners and friends. It had been a full six months before I realized Lucas' missing sister and my sister had been friends.

The coffee maker grows quiet and I fill a mug. Alexis is still asleep and not here to see, so I add too much sugar and cream. A few drops of vanilla, and it's almost as good as the froo-froo coffee I secretly prefer. Sipping the sweet elixir, I watch the front yard grow brighter.

Walker cries out from down the hall, cutting my early morning moments of solitude short. His huge smile when I enter his room blows the swirling thoughts of Crystal and murder from my mind. He stands in his crib, his pudgy hands reaching for me.

"Morning, buddy," I whisper to my son. "Let's not wake Mommy, okay?" Walker lays his head on my shoulder and grips my wet tank top. I grab a diaper off the changing table and sneak down the hall.

After a quick change into dry pants, I sit on the floor and watch Walker playing with his toys. He loves anything with wheels and pushes his favorite plastic police cruiser into my outstretched legs.

I pretend the small bump hurts like crazy and make a

big fuss. Walker laughs at my antics, pleased for some Daddy time.

"Come here," I say, pulling him onto my lap. He laughs and squirms to be released. I pick him up and hold him over my head. His adorable face beams at me as I fake drop him and he squeals with delight.

"I could wake up to this every morning," Alexis says behind us.

Hearing his mommy's voice, Walker squeals. I put him down and he skitters across the carpet on hands and knees.

"Sorry if we woke you," I say, smiling at my family and pushing myself up to the couch.

Alexis expertly scoops up Walker, then sits next to me, dropping a kiss on my cheek. Walker climbs from her lap to mine, then back again. I tickle his ribs and his squeals fill the living room.

"You're up early," Alexis says, noting my sweat-stained tank.

"I didn't sleep too well," I say suddenly serious.

"Worried she'll actually be there or that she won't?"

"Both. Either way, it's a loss. Either Gabby's wrong and all this is for nothing, or Crystal was actually murdered and hidden in someone else's grave." Walker senses playtime is over and climbs back on the floor to his toy cruiser.

"I'm surprised you got the court order at all."

"Lucas' dad has a friend that's a judge."

"How's Lucas handling all this?" Alexis curls against my shoulder.

"At first he was pretty shook up, but yesterday he seemed in a really good mood, so hard to tell."

Alexis snuggles closer, her sleep messed hair brushing against my cheek. "At least he has you."

I allow myself to enjoy the snuggle for another moment. "Speaking of all that I need to get going."

Used to my quick changes in mood, Alexis lets me go. "And take a shower," she says, sliding onto the floor to play with Walker. "You're all sweaty."

"You didn't mind last night," I tease.

She laughs and throws a plastic truck after me. "You're horrible."

For once, the unpredictable Indiana weather works to our advantage. All the snow has melted from the cemetery and the sunny day promises to be warmer. I string yellow tape in a perimeter around the area of the grave in question. Far across the cemetery, a couple visits another grave, taking advantage of the break in the weather. Besides them, the only action surrounds me.

A small backhoe sits nearby, the driver waiting impatiently to dig. Two uniformed officers help secure the scene. Lucas ducks under the yellow tape with a nod of greeting to the officers and joins me near the headstone.

"Hey," I say, not sure what words are appropriate at such an unusual event.

"Hey," he says back. He stares at the ground in front of the headstone, his back stiff. "My parents are coming if that's okay."

"Of course," I say. "There they are now."

Gregor Hartley strides with purpose across the cemetery. Deidre walks with her chin held so high it looks unnatural, a tight smile frozen on her face. Gregor nods at me and his son as he takes his place outside the tape.

Deidre's smile never wavers, but never reaches her eyes. She plants her feet solidly on the now mushy ground and fixes her eyes on a point in the distance.

"I'm not late, am I?" Gabby suddenly says behind me.

I turn in surprise. "Late? I didn't even know you were coming."

Lucas holds up the tape for her, and she ducks under. A snap of annoyance courses through me.

"I'm glad you're here," Lucas says to her, taking her hand in his, looking pointedly at me for my reaction.

I force my face to hide my surprise. "Whatever you want," I snap at Gabby. "As usual," I mutter under my breath, turning away from my partner and my sister holding hands.

The coroner arrives at the scene and I eagerly focus on her. "Ready for this?" Angelica Gomez asks with a hint of irritation. Her intelligent, dark eyes narrow on the bystanders. "Is this the family?"

Gomez barely reaches my chest in height, but she's hard and clever, her entire demeanor commands respect. "Yes, ma'am," I say contritely, hating myself for my reaction.

The tail of Gomez's usual french braid swings in an arc as she turns on Gabby and looks her up and down with sharp eyes. "What are you doing here?"

Gabby blanches under the intense scrutiny and a smile ticks up the corners of my mouth.

"She's with me," Lucas says.

"She's not police." Gomez says. "Behind the tape." The braid swings again as Gomez turns back to the job at hand. "Let's get this started," she says to the driver waiting on the backhoe.

The machine roars to life and the first scrape of dirt is removed. "Not too much," Gomez barks at the driver.

As the hole grows deeper and nothing is found but dirt and a few rocks, the tension around the grave mounts.

Lucas stands with Gabby and his parents behind the tape. I scan his face for a hint of the guilt Gabby thought she heard from Crystal. Anxiety is clear, but I don't sense guilt from him.

Gabby checks Lucas' face as well, seems relieved then looks back at the hole. Her anxiety seems more based on anticipation than dread.

Gregor Hartley wears an expression so like his son's it's unnerving. Deidre Hartley still wears her fake smile and empty eyes. The quivering of her lower lip is the only hint of true emotion.

The backhoe removes another scoop and Gomez turns her assessing eyes on me. "Sure she's in here?" she asks, shooting a meaningful look at Gabby.

"Gabby said she's here," I defend my sister.

"There she is!" Gabby suddenly shouts above the sound of the backhoe.

At the bottom of the hole, a bone peaks out of the dirt. The white surface bright against the damp earth.

Gomez shouts at the driver to stop digging and he turns off the machine.

The following silence is shattered by a scream.

Deidre Hartley's smile fights to remain on her face, but her mouth is open and screaming.

Chapter 15

Gabby

Lucas' hand in mine centers me as I watch the dirt scrape away from the grave. I hope my hand in his centers him as well. I can't imagine what emotions must be coursing through him. Gloves or no gloves, I've never been able to get a reading from him. That lack allows me to touch him freely, but I wish I could get inside his head right now.

Or maybe I don't. My own head is enough of a mess to deal with. I'm sure Crystal is under the dirt, but as the hole gets deeper a niggle of doubt begins to swirl.

I look at the small crowd watching the digging. All these people are here because of me. The responsibility weighs me down and I squeeze Lucas' hand harder.

He silently squeezes back.

The spit-fire of a coroner keeps sending me side glances, leaving no doubt as to her opinion of me and my abilities. "You're wasting everyone's time," her eyes tell me.

I lift my chin and ignore the silent jibe.

A moment later, Gomez is proved wrong.

The long white bone appears in the dirt and I flash back to the first bones I was called to touch.

I shake the thought away and screaming fills my ears. For a moment, I think the screaming comes from me.

Deidre Hartley collapses on the ground. "My daughter! My baby!" she wails.

Lucas drops my hand and rushes to his mother. Gregor Hartley cradles his wife. Lucas wraps them both in his arms.

I watch the display of family emotion in stunned silence.

Dustin touches my arm and I brace for harsh words. "Looks like you were right," he says with uncustomary gentleness. His hand remains on my arm as we watch the Hartleys lost in grief.

"McAllister," Gomez barks at my brother. "Get these people out of here. We have work to do."

Dustin's hand flinches, then drops to his side. "He's going to need you. Can you help get them home?"

I nod. "Can you call me later and tell me what you find out?"

"You already know more than we can find."

"What about Lucy?"

"Lucy Reed was killed by trauma to her head. Most likely caused by the hoof of her horse." Gomez interrupts our conversation. "You found her. You should know." The inflection on "know" mocks me.

"I *knew* Crystal was here," I snap at the woman.

Gomez eyes me critically. "You knew somehow," she says cryptically, turning back to her work, effectively dismissing me.

My entire body tenses at the accusation. Deidre's renewed wailing distracts me from jumping on the coroner and pulling on her long braid.

"Just take them home." Dustin rubs his hand across the short buzz cut of his hair. "Please."

"Come on, Mom," Lucas says to his mom. "We found her. Now, let's let them work."

"I'm sorry, man," Dustin says to his friend. Lucas nods and straightens his shoulders.

With Gregor on one side and Lucas on the other, they lead Deidre toward the parking area. I walk with the family, feeling like an interloper. They don't need me right now, but Dustin needs me gone. Crystal's remains must be removed and examined.

I've done all I can for her.

"I'm going to go with them," Lucas says as the men settle Deidre into Gregor's car.

"That's good." I touch his shoulder, offering what small comfort I can. "I'll catch up with you later?" I meant it as a statement, and hate the needy note of question that seeped out.

He takes my hand from his shoulder and squeezes it. "Of course."

After they drive away, I watch the yellow crime tape shimmering in the sun. The ugly tape is an abomination to the serenity of the cemetery.

"I'm so sorry," I whisper to Crystal.

I have two clients to fill my day and am happy about

the distractions. With one eye on my phone, hoping Lucas will call and another on the clock wishing it would tick faster, I make it through the day. The clients were simple readings on old items. Not a crime or cheating spouse in sight.

Deidre's pitiful cries echo in my memory. The mother's pain haunting. Another mother, Annette Reed is mourning the loss of a child today. The sad thoughts make me miss my own mother.

But Emily McAllister is in prison a few hundred miles away, out of reach until my next visit. What I really want is Grandma Dot to rub my back and tell me it will all be fine. I may have told Dustin I didn't need to run crying to Grandma all the time, but that was a lie.

I check the clock again. I want Grandma, not all her clients. The beauty shop will close soon and I can have her to myself.

Spinning the dial on the safe under the front counter, I shove the pile of cash my two clients paid today inside.

The gold coin I found at the shack catches my eye. Revealing my true feelings for Lucas and dealing with Crystal's exhumation had forced the coin from my mind.

I pluck the coin out of the safe and flip it in my gloved palm. The cross and coat of arms stamped on it are smudged and worn from the hundreds of years of its existence. Or are made to look old, and the coin's a fake.

That would make more sense. How could an authentic Spanish gold coin wind up under a dirty mattress in a shack in Indiana?

I pull off my left glove, then bow my head and say my

usual prayer. "God, let me see what needs to be seen."

The gold warms as I close my hand around it and close my eyes.

Anger, pain, greed, hope.

Vague impressions that mean nothing. Spanish coins like this were made from gold stolen from the natives. Stacks of coins were loaded onto ships to return to greedy lords in Spain. Some were lost on shipwrecks. Some remained here and used as currency. The exact history of this coin could be sordid and bloody or simply a piece of everyday life.

Even as sketchy as the vision appears, the layers of time are evident.

The coin is real.

I cling to the coin and open my mind again, desperate for a clue. With my eyes scrunched closed, I dig into the vision, sift through the flitting impressions.

Anger, pain, greed, hope.

Below that, *fear and betrayal.*

Irritated at the lack of answers, I toss the coin onto the counter with a clatter. It rocks on its edges then settles into silence. I stare at it, hoping inspiration will jump from the gold into my mind.

The coin just lays there.

Angry, I pull my glove on and shove the coin in my pocket. I slam the door of the safe and spin the dial to make sure it locks. Grandma's probably finishing up at the beauty shop.

I don't care if it makes me look like a child, I need my

Grandma.

A woman with beautifully styled hair opens the driver's door of the last car in Grandma's parking area. The last client of the afternoon.

I let myself into the kitchen door and the familiar smells of home wash over me. My shoulders soften and my body relaxes instantly. "Grandma, it's Gabby," I shout towards the sliding doors leading to the beauty shop.

Jet pushes his nose through a crack in the door, slides it open and scrambles across the floor. I scoop him into my arms and rub my cheek against his ear. "I missed you, too, buddy."

"Just finishing up," Grandma Dot calls from the shop.

I pour myself a tall glass of iced tea and play with Jet while I wait. I don't have to wait long.

Grandma Dot inspects me in her usual way. "Something's different about you."

"They found Crystal in the grave this morning."

Grandma touches my face, runs a finger over the scar in my eyebrow. "I heard. It's not that."

My cheeks burn hot under her scrutiny. I can never hide anything from her.

"I kissed Lucas," I say shyly.

Grandma claps her hands together in excitement. "About time," she exclaims. "I've been watching you two dance for years."

My cheeks burn even hotter. "Grandma, stop."

"Wait til I tell Mrs. Mott," Grandma crows. "We've had a bet going. If you had waited until after Christmas, you would have cost me money."

"You're betting on my love life?" I try to sound annoyed, but it comes out amused.

"We old ladies have to find our excitement somewhere." She shrugs one shoulder. "So, how was it?"

I laugh out loud at this. "I'm not telling you that."

"Ooh, that means it was good."

"Please, stop."

"Fine. Suit yourself." Grandma fixes her own glass of tea and joins me at the table. "If you're not going to dish about Lucas, tell me how this morning went."

The happy mood turns sour. "It sucked."

"We already knew what they'd find. Couldn't have been worse than the other day."

"The other day I didn't have to watch Crystal's mom scream in agony." I sip my tea and avoid Grandma's eyes.

"That bad?" Grandma sips from her glass. "Deidre Hartley was always a drama queen."

"Grandma, don't talk like that," I scold.

"Well, I feel sorry for her, of course. But she's the type who will milk this for all it's worth."

"You're awful."

"She's awful. I never understood how a pain-in-the-butt like her has such a nice son." She shoots me a sly look.

"I'm not talking about Lucas and me right now."

"Romance is more fun than death." Grandma scoops Jet onto her lap. "Enough death going around."

"I'm sorry about Lucy. I know she and Annette were clients of yours."

"Annette's a mess, as you can imagine. Lucy was her

127

whole world, and she was taken away." Grandma stares out the window and I wonder if she's thinking about my mom, her only child, taken away from her. But Emily is still alive. Lucy is not.

"The coroner said that Lucy's death was apparently caused by the horse hitting her in the head."

Grandma sighs heavily. "Annette called earlier and told me that they released Lucy's body. She asked me to do her hair tomorrow for the funeral."

"Do Lucy's hair?"

"I've done that kind of thing before. Unfortunately, as my clients have gotten older, I've done it more often than I'd like."

"Isn't it hard on you?"

"It's not easy, but they deserve it. It's a final way for me to honor them. You know what I mean?"

I think about this and sip more tea. "I guess that makes sense. I'm sorry you have to go through it, though. I never knew you did that."

"I don't tell you everything." Grandma tries for a joke to lighten the mood. "I can have secrets, you know."

I smile gratefully at the effort and play along. "Old lady secrets. Yuck."

"You're a brat."

"And that's why you love me," I retort.

Grandma rubs at a scratch on the wooden table, "What are you going to do about Crystal?" she asks seriously.

"Not sure what I can do," I say. "I have no idea who strangled her."

"But you can find out. It's what you do."

"It's what Dustin and Lucas do."

"You can help. You know you're going to."

I finger the coin in my pocket through the fabric of my jeans. "I tried the other day."

"And?" Grandma's eyes light up with interest.

"I had a client tell me about how Crystal and her friends used to hang out at a shack by the river on the Hartley property."

"Interesting," Grandma prompts. "What did you find there?"

"How do you know I went?"

"Because you would go and snoop as soon as you heard about it." She sits back in her chair, prepared to listen to a story.

"Fine. I did go snoop, as you say. The place was pretty much falling down. Groundhogs have dug all over the place. I found this."

I slap the coin on the kitchen table, gratified by Grandma's intake of surprised breath.

"A gold coin?" She picks it up and inspects the engravings. "This is Spanish, from hundreds of years ago," she says in awe.

"And it's real. At least, it felt old, really old, when I tried to get a reading off it."

"What else did you see from it?"

"Nothing. Trust me, I wish I could see something that would tell me what a very expensive coin like this was doing buried under that shack."

Grandma turns the coin over and over in her hand, deep in thought. "It looks familiar."

"It's in all the pirate movies," I point out.

"Not that. I've held one of these in my hand before."

My ears perk up at that nugget. "Where, when?"

She shakes her head. "I don't know. When you've been around as much as I have, you see a lot of things." She places the coin back on the table and slides it to me. "Do you think it has something to do with Crystal's murder?"

I return the coin to my pocket. "Not sure. Maybe the shack means nothing. Lucy used to hang out there with the other kids, too. Seems there might be a connection."

"But Lucy died in an accident," Grandma says.

"I talked to her right before that. She had something she wanted to tell me. She said I was a life-saver." I swallow hard. "Then she died. I didn't save her life."

Grandma pats my hand. "Gabriella, you had no way of knowing what was going to happen to her. She tended those horses every day for years. Horses can be unpredictable."

"That's another thing. Where did she get the money for a place as nice as that? Did she win the lottery and I don't know about it?"

"Good at business?" Grandma ventures.

"Did mousy little Lucy Reed seem like a sharp businesswoman to you? You knew her better than I did."

"She talked a lot about her horses," Grandma muses. "She definitely knew her stuff."

I sigh heavily. "I'm grasping at straws. I just don't know who would kill Crystal back then, or why. I should have been a better friend. I don't really know anything about her life after we drifted apart."

"Then talk to the ones who knew her best. Like her handsome brother."

"I've been trying to give him space."

"Maybe it's not space that he needs right now. He needs you."

I look at my silent cell phone. "I've been waiting for him to call all day. He went home with his parents and I didn't want to intrude."

"Gabriella." Grandma shakes her head sadly. "If you sit around and wait for things to happen, nothing ever will. No wonder it took you two so long to realize you were in love."

"Who said anything about being in love?" I ask defensively.

"You've been in love with that boy for a long time and he's been in love with you. Oh, youth is wasted on the young. Call him, go to him. Do something instead of sit here and wait for your life to happen."

"But we just dug up his dead sister this morning. He should be with his family."

"You are his family." She looks at me intently. "As I said, romance is more fun than death. I used to tell Dustin the same thing when he first became a cop. There will always be more crime, more cases. You can't put your life on hold for each one, or your life will be over and you will have missed it."

I cock my head at her, "How'd you get so smart?"

"I was born smart, sweetheart," she quips and stands up. "Now get out of here. Go console that man of yours."

131

"Man of mine, that sounds strange." I stand and push my chair in.

"Get used to it." Grandma leans in for a hug. "I'm so pleased for you," she says near my ear. "About time you had some happiness."

"I really am happy, despite all the other bad stuff going on."

She releases me and shoves me towards the door. "Cling to the happy and let the bad stuff fall where it will," she calls after me.

The cold bites my cheeks as I make my way back to my car, but my chest still feels warm from Grandma's hug.

Chapter 16

Gabby

Lucas' pleasure at hearing from me makes me think Grandma was right and he'd been waiting for my call as I waited for his. He's spent all day with his parents and quickly invites me over.

Maverick, the Great Dane's, excitement when I walk through the door matches Lucas' expression. "Thanks for coming. Been a long day here," Lucas says, simultaneously kissing my cheek and pushing Maverick off of me.

"I wasn't sure what I should do, so I stayed at work then went to Grandma's."

"Well, you're here now, that's what matters." Once Maverick stops jumping on me, Lucas pulls me against him. I sink into him eagerly, breathe in his scent, a mixture of his cologne and stress.

"You feel good," I mumble into his chest.

"So do you," he answers.

"Are you going to let the girl inside the house or just paw at her all night?" Gregor Hartley interrupts.

I pull away quickly, my face on fire.

"I see you took my advice," Gregor says slyly. "Smart girl."

Lucas shoots me a questioning look. "Don't ask," I mouth to him.

"Come on in here to the kitchen," Gregor says, motioning me down the hall. "Are you hungry? Food has already started arriving."

My stomach rumbles loudly. "I could eat," I say casually.

"Offerings of food are a social convention that I've never understood." Gregor takes a plate out of a cabinet in the spacious kitchen and hands it to me. "Makes people feel included in your grief without being too intrusive, I suppose. The action of making and delivering food to the bereaved gives people the semblance of control in an uncontrollable situation."

I blink at the unexpected lecture. "Dad, Gabby doesn't need a lesson right now," Lucas comes to my rescue.

Gregor pulls open a drawer. "Right. Sorry. I don't know what I'm saying. Forgive me." He stares into the open drawer for a long moment. "A fork, right. That's what you need." He takes a fork then slams the drawer shut too hard.

I exchange a worried glance with Lucas. "Why don't you sit back down, Dad."

I fill a plate with food then join Gregor at the table. Lucas leans against the counter, watching his dad with worried eyes. "You have a lovely home." It's the only thing I can think of to say. "This kitchen is to die for."

134

I instantly regret my choice of words and shove a bite of casserole into my mouth to shut myself up.

"Deidre designed it," Gregor says vaguely, patting Maverick's huge head. "Not that she's much of a cook."

I suddenly realize Deidre isn't with us and look around. "Where's your mom?" I ask Lucas.

"She was very upset this morning and went to bed when we got home. She hasn't come down since." Lucas looks at the doorway that leads to the hall. "Maybe we should check on her?" he asks, a flutter of worry crossing his face.

"I'll go," Gregor says instantly. "Leave you two love birds to it. Come, Maverick." His odd change of mood startles, but maybe grief will do that to you.

Lucas takes the chair his father vacated. "I had some of that earlier," he motions to the food on my plate. "Good, isn't it?"

My mouth is full, so I only nod. I search my mind for something to say as I chew. No words seem adequate, so I slide my hand on top of Lucas'. The quiet of the kitchen surrounds us, the hum of the refrigerator a soothing backdrop to the intimate moment.

"I'm sorry about Crystal," I say finally. "I can't imagine what this must feel like to you and your parents."

"A bit surreal," he concedes.

"Do you want to talk about it?"

"Dad and I've been not talking about it all day. We've made calls to other family and friends. We have an appointment at the funeral home set. We've talked about a lot of things today. But not the one thing I want to discuss."

"What's that?" I set my fork down on the table, no longer interested in eating.

"Who the hell killed her?" he says hotly. "She didn't bury herself there."

"Has Dustin figured anything out yet?"

Lucas leans back in his chair in agitation. "I talked to him a while ago. He says I can't be part of the investigation. Too close and all that crap."

"Leave it to my brother to follow the rules," I gripe.

"He's right, of course. But I don't care." He runs a hand across his short hair. "I feel powerless and shut out."

"There's nothing stopping us from thinking and talking," I point out. "Let's start with what we know."

"You're teaching me how to investigate?" He gives me a wry smile.

"Not teaching, just guiding." I lean towards him across the table. "Annette's father died a few days before Crystal ran away. That much we know for sure. So why did Crystal run away in the first place? You've never really told me that part."

Lucas looks across the kitchen and back in time. The whirring of the fridge stops suddenly and it's too quiet in the kitchen. "The usual reasons, I guess. She had started running with a bad crowd, started getting into trouble, that kind of thing. She and mom were always fighting."

He stands up suddenly and gets himself a can of soda from the fridge. "It was just after we graduated, were you back from college for the summer?"

"I was back in River Bend, but I wasn't home a lot.

136

You know how it is, catching up with all the friends you haven't seen in so long."

I actually have no idea what that's like, but don't tell him that.

"Anyway, Crystal was young and dumb and ready to start her life. When Mom said she and Crystal got in a fight and that Crystal left, I honestly wasn't that surprised. Hurt that she didn't say good-bye or ever contact me again, but not surprised."

"Except she didn't go anywhere. She was killed," I say as gently as possible. "So where did she go before that?"

He sips his soda. "I have no idea. At first, we figured she'd calm down and come home eventually. I really didn't give it too much thought." He sips again. "What a horrible brother I am. I didn't even know anything was wrong. I just figured she was okay and went on with my own life." He slams the can on the counter and soda splashes onto his hand. "Crap, what a mess." He shakes the soda off his hand into the sink.

I cross the kitchen and hand him a towel. "You had no way of knowing," I soothe. "None of us did."

He sighs heavily. "Someone did. The man who killed her."

"We will figure this out." I take the towel from him and wipe at the spilled soda.

"What did you see?" he asks.

I freeze in the act of wiping the counter. I don't want to tell him. It's bad enough I had to live through her death, her brother doesn't need to hear the gory details.

"She was strangled," I hedge.

"You saw more than that." He turns me to face him. "I need to know. Tell me everything you saw."

I blink a few times.

Honest, just be honest.

"She couldn't breathe. That's what I felt the most, her need for air. She knew whoever was doing it, because she felt betrayed."

I search my memory of the vision. Every sensation is burned into me, but explaining is difficult. It's like trying to describe a dream you had. You can see it clearly in your mind, but it's hard to make sense of it to someone else.

"Anything else? You said she was thinking of me."

"She was kind of begging for you to save her. She said something about not telling, that she promised not to tell. She thought about the necklace you gave her and that it was cutting into her neck. There was a smell, too. Some sort of perfume or cologne."

I say the words as gently as possible, but his face crumbles.

"The necklace I gave her?" he chokes on the words.

I place my hand on his shoulder, "I'm so sorry this is painful."

He crushes me to him suddenly, his face hot against my temple, his body shaking. The fridge kicks back on, but the hum isn't loud enough to cover the sound of his pain.

I cling to him, offering whatever comfort my embrace will give. He takes a shuddering breath and pushes me away.

"Crying about it won't bring her back." He turns away from me to wash his face at the kitchen sink.

"I've cried plenty," I tell him. "It does help."

He tears a paper towel off the roll hanging under a cabinet and blows his nose loudly. He still hasn't looked at me. In all the years I've known him, he's been the strong one, the rock, the one who holds me when I lose it. Seeing him torn down by grief makes my heart ache, but also fills me with a sense of purpose. He trusts me to let down his guard, if even for a moment. No one's ever trusted me like that.

"So," he says sharply and turns. "What's our next step? What else do we know?"

The vulnerability that consumed him moments ago hardens into resolve. His eyes narrow and his lips push together. I yearn to smooth the harsh expression away, but what he needs is answers.

"I heard from a client that Crystal and her friends liked to hang out at that shack down by the river."

"Which explains your appearance at the bridge the other day." A touch of a smile flitters across his face. My lips tingle remembering our kisses. "I forgot about that place. Did you find anything or sense something?"

"Not sure if it's important, but I found this." I pull the coin out of my pocket and hand it over.

"A gold coin?" He inspects it the same way Grandma did earlier.

"Does it mean anything to you?"

He flips it in his palm. "No. You found this at the shack?"

"Yeah, and a bunch of empty bottles and beer cans."

He flips the coin a few more times, searches it desperately like it will offer up answers.

The scratching of his claws on the floor precedes Maverick's bounding entry into the kitchen. "Maverick, slow down," a female voice snaps at him.

Lucas pushes the coin into his pocket. "Don't tell her," he whispers quickly. "Don't get her hopes up until we know something."

Maverick knocks into the table in his excitement and a chair clatters to the floor. "Good Lord, dog," Deidre Hartley grumbles. "Stop breaking every…." Seeing me in her kitchen, Deidre stops in mid-sentence. "Come on Mav, honey. Let's go outside," she says cheerily, opening the back patio door for him.

Maverick darts into the cold. "That boy has so much energy." Deidre slides the door closed and watches out the glass. She pulls her robe closer around her.

"Mom, you remember Gabby McAllister," Lucas says politely.

Deidre turns and says breezily, "Of course I do." Her face nearly cracks from the smile she beams on me. "How wonderful to see you again."

"Nice to see you, too, Mrs. Hartley." I pick up the fallen chair to give my nervous hands something to do.

"I didn't know we had company or I would have dressed." She cinches the belt of her robe tighter around her already small waist.

"You look fine, Mom. Gabby just stopped by to see how we were doing."

Deidre locks her strange smile on me. "How nice." I'm fixated by her over-white teeth flashing in her pale face. Nothing about my presence is nice to her right now.

Flustered, I say, "Uh, yeah," then turn to Lucas. "I'm going to go. You need to spend some time with your mom."

"Gabby, you don't have to go on my account," Deidre croons. "I'm sure my son would like you to stay." The emphasis on *my son* doesn't go unnoticed by me, but Lucas is oblivious.

"I've got to go," I say to Lucas. "I'm so sorry about your loss," I offer the platitude to Deidre.

"I'm sure you are," she says cryptically, the creepy smile still on her face.

Lucas follows me to the door and I hesitate with my hand on the doorknob. "Is your mom okay?" I can't keep from asking.

He looks down the hall towards the kitchen. "Why?"

"She seems, I don't know, odd." Confusion crosses his face. I hurry on, "Probably just the strain of the day."

"This day's sucked for all of us," he says sadly. "Oh, your coin." He pulls the gold from his pocket.

"It's not actually mine. I found it on your property."

"Keep it. It might help us."

I put the coin back in my pocket then push up on my toes to kiss his cheek. The stubble there pricks my lips, but the heat of his skin feels marvelous. "Call you tomorrow," I say then slip out the door.

My lips carry the memory of his stubble against them.

Chapter 17

Grandma Dot

I follow the funeral director down the stairs and through a long hall. Lucy's body waits for me in the workroom. My brave words to Gabriella last night about how doing the hair of the dead is a tribute to them replays through my mind. Honor and tribute, yes. But it doesn't make it easy.

"We've already dressed her and gotten her ready," the funeral director says, his demeanor completely professional and calm.

Inside, I want to scream. "Thank you," I answer politely, keeping my eyes locked on him instead of looking at Lucy's lifeless face.

"I'll be upstairs if you need anything." He hesitates, watching me. Probably wondering why I'm here instead of just letting them fix her curls.

I give him a tight smile and set my bag on a counter. "Thank you," I say again, not so politely this time. I want him to leave. I want to do this for Lucy – alone. Then get out of here.

He nods solemnly and shuts the door behind him with a gentle click.

It's just Lucy and me now. At least as far as I can see. I try not to think about the other unfortunate bodies behind the metal doors lining one wall.

Stealing my nerve, I finally look at the young woman on the table. The funeral home did a good job on her. You'd have to look very closely to see the injuries to her face.

I don't want to look that close.

"Just you and me, kid," I say to Lucy, trying to lighten my mood.

I pull the curling iron out of my bag and plug it into an outlet on the floor under the prep table. Her perm is recent, so her curls don't need too much work. A few touches of the curling iron and some backcombing and Lucy should look like she always did.

I wait for the curling iron to heat up and think about the young woman before me. Most of the people I've done funeral hair for have been older clients. Ones who've lived full lives.

Lucy's life was cut short. She never got married. Never had children. She's the same age as Gabriella and Dustin.

"Don't go there," I tell myself. "This is about Lucy, not you."

I test the iron, deciding it's hot enough. Taking a section of hair into my fingers, I close the curling iron and twist.

A shock shoots up my arm.

Startled, I drop the iron. It singes against her heavy restoration make-up and I snatch it back, releasing the curl.

"What the?" I inspect the iron, looking for a short or an exposed wire. Anything that would have shocked me.

The iron is in perfect working order.

Cautiously, I lift another section of hair.

The shock comes before I even get the hair on the iron.

I drop the iron and it clatters on the hard floor. The noise loud in the silent room.

Lucy's body lies still. Her eyes permanently closed. A tiny black spot from dropping the iron on her face mars the smooth work of the funeral home.

With the tip of my finger, I smudge the makeup to cover the mark.

Pain. Sharp pain.

 I jump away from her body. Confused and scared.

And curious.

I touch her face again, prepared this time.

Pain. Sharp pain in my head.

Lucy's pain wracks through my head. A sharp strike just behind my ear. I rub my hair, push against my skull.

Bending lower to her body, I peak behind her ear. I could turn her head to get a better look, but I don't want to touch her again.

I have to look closely, but a section of her skull is misshapen, repaired, but misshapen.

"What are you trying to tell me?" I ask her lifeless body. The damage to her skull could have been caused by the horse that trampled her. The pain I felt from her was overwhelming, but concentrated in one small spot.

"If I had Gabriella's abilities, I could hear what you're telling me."

Getting an idea, I dig in my bag for my phone. Gabriella knows how to do this.

It takes forever for Gabriella to arrive. I spend the time leaning against the wall farthest from Lucy. I have no interest in feeling her pain in my head again. No interest in touching her.

I promised Annette I'd do her hair, but I just can't. The funeral home will have to do it. I don't care if I look like a coward. I can't live through her death.

At one point, the pious director checks in on me. "Everything okay?" He must be curious why it's taking so long and why I'm far from Lucy, but his face is blank.

"I'm waiting for my granddaughter."

His eyebrows raise a fraction of an inch.

"She's bringing me a tool I need." I force myself to sound assured, in control. "Please bring her here when she arrives."

I catch the faintest expression on his face before he closes the door. "Amateur," his face says clearly.

The next time the door opens, Gabriella walks in slowly.

"Grandma?" she asks to the room, not seeing me leaning against the wall near the door.

"I'm here," I step towards her.

"What in the world is going on?" Her eyes dart to Lucy

and back to me. She shakes her head in confusion.

"Did you ever touch Lucy when you found her?" I ask.

"I didn't have the chance." Her face clouds. "Why?" she asks, suddenly wary.

"I was trying to do her hair, and I felt something." I look at Lucy. "Something bad."

"Well she was killed," Gabriella says. I appreciate that she doesn't question my feeling something. Her belief gives me strength. For a split second, I understand what it must be like for her. Knowing things, seeing things, but no one to believe you.

"Not like that," I hedge. "Can you?"

"Can I touch her?" Gabriella darts her eyes at Lucy again. Fear flickers across her face, then courage. My love for her grows in that instant.

"Just see if I'm right."

"About?"

"I don't think the horse killed her."

The words drop like heavy water in the silence, spread across the room.

Gabriella pulls off her gloves and strides to Lucy. She bows her head and mumbles. "Lord let me see what you need me to see." Her left hand hovers over Lucy's forehead and she looks at me. "Guard the door. I don't want anyone to see this."

I stand in front of the door and she drops her hand to Lucy.

Her chin flops to her chest and her knees weaken. She doesn't fall, but leans heavily against the prep table. She shakes her head and moans, "Don't. No, don't."

I hate to see her like that. My precious Gabriella reliving a woman's murder, feeling her pain. I rush over and pull her to me, wrapping her in my arms.

She leans heavily against me, shaking violently. "Come back, Gabriella. Come back."

Her shaking stops, but she clings, sniffling into my sweater.

"You were right," she says, straightening. "She was murdered. By a hammer to the head." She swallows a few times before continuing. "She was in the stall when someone snuck up and hit her. They must have shut the stall door and let the horse finish her off."

"Oh no," I breathe.

"Left her for me to find." A visible shudder courses through her.

I hate myself for forcing her to go through this. "I'm sorry I made you come."

She looks at Lucy again. "I should have seen it before. Or been there to stop it from happening in the first place. It's the least I can do for her now."

Two soft raps on the door and the director looks in on us. "I hate to push you, but it's not good for Ms. Reed to be out so long. Are you almost finished?"

Gabriella turns her head from the director and wipes her face with the sleeve of her coat. "I've got to talk to Dustin," she says. With her eyes on the floor and hidden from the director, she sneaks out.

I glance at Lucy with trepidation, then touch her hair. No visions, no pain. Whatever she needed to say, she told Gabriella. "I'll be right out," I tell the director.

I retrieve the forgotten curling iron from where it fell under the prep table and get to work on Lucy's hair. Her perm is recent and the curls only need a little help.

"She's just asleep," I repeat under my breath, working as quickly as possible. "She's just asleep."

Chapter 18

Gabby

Emotions pummel me as I escape up the steps and burst into the cold air. Pride that I was able to help Grandma. Pain that I felt from Lucy. Anger that someone killed her. Confusion at what to do with the information.

One word swirls to the top of the boiling mess of emotions.

Stupid.

Stupid, stupid, stupid. You stupid girl, you should have known when you found her. You should have known. Lucy asked for your help and you just left her there without even trying.

"Stupid, stupid, stupid," I yell inside the privacy of my Charger, pounding my hand against the steering wheel with each word. Slamming until my hand aches.

Images of Lucy's bloody face cradled against my chest mix with the sterilized face of her prepared body. She's dead. She's gone.

I let it happen.

My tires squeal as I pull out of the funeral home parking lot. Not a dignified escape that the location deserves.

Dignity has never been my strong suit.

Once I get myself under enough control to not scream into the phone, I call Dustin.

"Lucy Reed was murdered," I blurt as soon as he answers. He sighs heavily in response. I'm not in the mood for his attitude. "You can ask Grandma Dot. She's the one who got the vision first. She felt it when she was doing Lucy's hair. I just confirmed it."

"Two psychic visions don't make a confirmation." His exasperation rankles.

"You know, Dustin, I've had enough of this crap from you," I snap. "You can either get on board with this psychic thing and or you can lose me forever. I'm tired of trying to please you. I am what I am. Deal with it."

I've shocked him into silence. Shocked myself.

While he struggles to form a response, my tattoo starts to tingle.

Lucy's house.

I rub my arm. I'll go, but I need to hear Dustin's response first.

"How?" he finally says. "How was she killed?"

That was easy. This honesty thing is really working out. "Someone hit her on the head then left her for the horse to finish off."

"Crap." He blows out air in frustration. "What am I supposed to do with that?"

The tingle in my arm grows stronger.

"We have a bigger problem," I tell him. "Lucy and Crystal were murdered by the same person."

152

"I'm going to regret this, but how do you know for sure?"

"I smelled them. In Crystal's vision, I smelled perfume like flowery soap. I smelled the same thing with Lucy."

"Psychic smells now? Gabby, come on."

"Get on board or jump off. I'm going to Lucy's house. It has something to tell me."

I hang up before he can talk me out of it. If I'd paid more attention, I could have saved Lucy. She's not here to press breaking and entering charges, and, if I'm right, it won't matter in the end.

The horses in the pasture are startled away from the fence when I plow up Lucy's driveway. I wonder absently who's taking care of them now, but push the thought away and park the car. The silence of the house feels imposing in the expanse of Lucy's glorious property. My blood sings with adrenaline after my phone confrontation with Dustin, but I also feel lighter. I've wanted to say those words to Dustin since we were teens, but always held my tongue. I'm done with pretending I'm normal. My brother can love me or not.

Lucas loves me. Grandma loves me.

Dustin can make his own choice.

The chandelier on her front porch creaks ominously above my head. The thick wood of the door blocks my entrance. I try the knob, but no surprise, it's locked. I need to get into the house. My tattoo repeats *Lucy's house. Lucy's house.*

"I'm here, now give me a minute," I yell at my arm.

I ram my shoulder into the heavy door the way they

do on TV. I bounce off with only a sore shoulder for my troubles.

Rubbing my arm, I survey my options. A picture window elegantly graces the front of the house. Glass is easy to break.

I find a suitable rock in the front flower beds and raise it high to throw against the window.

An approaching car makes me freeze.

Dustin's here.

I drop the rock guiltily as he rushes down the sidewalk. He looks at the rock by my feet.

"Breaking the window?"

"I need to get inside," I say meekly.

He leans against a column holding up the second story balcony, crosses his arms on his chest. He strives to look casual, but he practically sizzles with tension.

"Can we talk before you commit a crime?"

"What do you want to talk about?" I hedge, kicking the rock with the toe of my hiking boot.

"Don't play coy," he snaps, then continues in a more controlled voice. "I realize that your visions are almost always right. I'll grant you that. I'll even go along with this matching smell theory of yours."

I try to respond, but he holds up a hand to stop me. "Let me finish, or I'll never say this." He looks over Lucy's land, gathering his thoughts. "Do you remember that basketball game from high school?"

His question takes me by surprise, but I play along. "The night the whole town turned on me, but I saved all those lives?" He shoots me a warning look at my sarcasm.

"Sorry. Yes, I remember."

"Do you know why I was so upset?"

I'd never thought about it, was just hurt by his dismissal. "No."

"You didn't care about looking foolish, being seen as a freak." I flinch at the word, but he doesn't notice. "All you cared about was saving everyone. That's how you've always been. Right now, for instance, you have to know what this psychic stuff sounds like. You have to know saying the house has something to tell you sounds crazy."

I nod silently.

"But you don't care. You just want to help."

"Wherever you're going with this, he'd better hurry or I'll hit you with this rock." I toe the rock he saw me drop.

"I'm jealous of you, Gabby," he states.

"Come on, I'm not in the mood for this."

"I'm serious. At that game, you saved everyone and you didn't care how you looked. Do you know why I became a cop? I wanted to help people like you do." The admission seems to weigh him down. "After that night, I wanted to matter, to be someone. So I became a cop."

"But you've always made fun of me," I protest.

He pushes off the column and runs his hand over his short hair. "You and Grandma always left me out. I was jealous of your special gift and I hated myself for being jealous. So I focus on facts and details. Then you start solving crimes with this psychic stuff. Think how that makes me feel? My whole life's dedicated to gathering facts to solve crimes. All you have to do is touch something."

My head spins with his honesty. "So you don't hate me?" I sound like a child, but I don't care.

"Only sometimes." His face breaks into a smile.

"That's okay. Sometimes I hate you, too." I return the smile, happy to be drifting back to normal ground.

"If you tell anyone what I just said, I'll deny it. That includes Lucas. I have a reputation to uphold."

"My reputation is shot, I can do what I want." I tiny giggle escapes my nervous lips.

"Another reason I'm jealous," he bumps my shoulder with his and bends to pick up the rock. "So we're okay, right?"

"We're good. Thank you for talking to me."

He bounces the rock in his palm a few times. "Too bad I got here too late to stop you from breaking this window." He hurls the rock and glass shatters.

"I can't believe you just did that," I squeal. "What a rebel."

"Shut up and get in there. You said this house has something to tell you. Let's find it."

I've never loved Dustin more than I do at this moment. The emotion is unfamiliar but welcome. I punch him on the shoulder, "Me first." Careful of the broken glass, I climb into Lucy's dining room. Dustin hesitates outside. "You coming, rebel?" I finally ask.

"Crap," he says, then throws his leg over the window sill.

Broken glass crunching under our feet and the police tools jangling on Dustin's belt are the only sounds in the cavernous house. A massive dining table fills the room.

156

The highly polished wood pristinely reflects the sunlight. Not a mark or scratch on the surface, so different from Grandma Dot's well-used table. Lucy's table sits eight, but appears to never have been eaten on. The shiny surface makes me sad. Lucy obviously had money, but no one to share it with.

"What exactly are we looking for?" Dustin asks.

I listen for a hint from my arm, but now that I'm inside, it's as quiet as the empty house. "Not sure. I was just told to come here." I snap my head in his direction, sure he'll catch the admission. I've never explained to Dustin about the messages I get from my tattoo. I once trusted Preston with the information, and he promptly left me.

Dustin watches my reaction. "I was honest with you, why don't you be completely honest with me? We both know there's more to your abilities than you tell me. How did the house talk to you?"

He seems sincere. Cautious, but sincere.

I plunge ahead and pull off my coat, drag the sleeve of my sweater up so he can see my tattoo. I look at the delicate black cross on my skin then look at him.

"You're tattoo? I don't understand."

"When I need to know something or do something, my tattoo tingles. Then I hear words in my head." I pull my sleeve down and zip myself back into my coat.

His eyes narrow in thought, making connections, analyzing my words. "Is that what happened in the corn maze that time?"

I nod, my emotions ping-ponging from hope he

157

understands to shame that he won't.

"And why you went into that church?"

I nod again.

"Good Lord, Gabby. You're really a mess aren't you?" His words would sting, except for the tinge of concern under them.

"I told you it's not easy to be me," I sass, turning on my heel and heading into Lucy's kitchen. I don't want to discuss the tattoo. He knows and he didn't run out the door. That's enough for right now.

"Any tingles now?" he says close behind me, without a trace of his usual sarcasm.

I stare at the granite-topped island in the middle of the kitchen. A pile of papers and a purple felt bag are arranged on the counter. "I don't need a tingle. I found what I am looking for."

The top paper on the stack is a print out of a coin. A gold coin, similar to the one locked in the safe at my shop.

Chapter 19

Gabby

Dustin flips through the pages, more print outs of coins. Some gold and Spanish, some silver ones, some that look like they could be Roman. "What's all this? Was she a coin collector or something?"

"Lucy was expecting me, said she had something to tell me. I must have been about this stuff." I pick up the purple felt bag, surprised by the weight and the clink of metal inside. I open the tiny gold-colored tie and peer inside. Several coins glitter in the dark of the felt. I pour them out on the countertop.

"Holy cow, that's a lot of coins." Dustin touches a couple, slides them around on the granite. "If these are real, they're very expensive."

"They're real," I state firmly. "I found one at a shack on the Hartleys' property too," I explain about why I went to the shack and what I found.

Dustin digests the information with the same intense face he wore when thinking about my tattoo. He steps back from the counter suddenly. "Don't touch anything.

This will need to be processed for evidence."

I hold up my always gloved hands. "Got that covered," I smile. "Can I take pictures?"

"We already broke in, why not finish the job?" he says.

With my cell phone, I snap shots of the coins and each paper Lucy had ready for me. The headline on an article she printed catches my eye. "Priceless coin collection stolen from treasure museum," I read to Dustin.

He snatches the paper from my hand, ignoring his own warning about touching them. "This is dated a few months before Crystal went missing."

"This was in South Carolina," I point out. "What would that have to do with River Bend?"

"What does any of this have to do with anything? Did you get a reading off the coin you found?" He asks hopefully.

"Just that it's real."

His shoulders sag and his face scrunches with thought. "First things first. I need to talk to the coroner about Lucy, confirm what you said about the injuries to her head." He whistles between his teeth. "Gomez is going to tear me a new one for this. She doesn't like her work being questioned."

"Either do I," I warn.

"Back off, I'm on your side. I just have to do it correctly, follow the facts. You better take your pictures and get out of here. Someone will have to come take care of the horses at least a few times a day. Will screw up the case if you're caught here.

I snap photos furiously and ask, "What about you?"

"I'll say you told me about the murder and got curious so I drove out here. The window was already broken, vandals, or something." His voice is vague as he thinks. "I climbed in to check things out and found all this."

"Will everyone fall for that?"

"I'm head detective," he shrugs. "With an impeccable reputation, remember?" He gives me a grin, a true grin I remember from our childhood, before Dad disappeared and our worlds shattered.

On impulse, I throw my arms around my brother. "You're a good brother," I whisper, inhaling the scent of his cologne. Something warm with an undercurrent of outdoors. It oddly reminds me of home.

Under his heavy protective vest and the assortment of tools on his belt, he feels stiff. A moment later, he relaxes and pats my back. "Get out of here."

That pat was the sweetest gesture I've received from him in years. Before emotion can catch me, I let him go and hurry past the massive, lonely dining table and climb out the window into the cold.

I want to call Lucas and tell him what we found. I pull up his info, but my finger hovers over the icon to connect the call. What can I tell him at this point? I still don't know what happened to his sister. He was going with his parents to the funeral home to plan for Crystal's service and burial. Thankfully Deidre chose an up-scale funeral home closer to Fort Wayne, not the local one where Lucy is.

Scrolling through my contacts, I don't hesitate to

connect to my friend, Haley. I check the clock as the phone rings. Our breaks at the call-center were tightly scheduled. If I'm lucky, Haley will be on her break now.

I get lucky and she answers. "Is this the famous Gabby McAllister I saw on TV?" she teases.

Her happy demeanor soothes the tension of what I need to ask her. "Not sure if I'm famous, but I'm available for autographs," I tease back, feeling a bit self-conscious. Goofing around with friends is a skill I never learned.

Haley doesn't seem to notice my awkwardness. "I saw you found another dead person buried in someone else's grave. That's wild."

I've purposely avoided watching the news and whatever crazy theories Lacey Aniston wants to spread. "Did she make me look bad?"

"Just a little veiled innuendo that you must have known that girl was there. Don't worry, no one believes anything Lacey says."

"Some people do. I heard she got a job offer in Indianapolis and will be leaving soon."

"Must be sleeping with that producer, too. She's a busy woman." I enjoy the sarcasm and insults to Lacey, but I have other things on my mind.

"Are you still doing any hacking?" I change subjects abruptly.

"The term hacking is so last week," Haley says. "But if you mean do I occasionally spend too much time researching odd tidbits of information on the internet, then, yes."

"If I send you a bunch of pictures of stolen coins, do you think you could find out more about them?"

"Sounds juicy, but if you already know they're stolen, what do you need me for?"

"Anything you can find. I'm not sure they are all stolen. I'll send you what I have and take a look, can you?"

"Does this have to do with the girl you found?"

"I'm not sure about that either. That's why I need you."

"Even juicier," she coos. "Sure, I'll do it. Now, how's that hot detective of yours?"

Dishing with a friend about my love life is another thing I have no practice in. "He's mine now, officially," I say shyly.

Her squeal of delight hurts my ears. "I knew it! Tell me everything."

"I'm not going to tell you everything," I laugh along with her excitement. "We've just kissed a few times. And he's taking me to an event at the antique car museum tonight."

"Fancy. Are you going to wear that blue dress from your party?"

"I guess. It's the only dress I own."

"And it looks so good with your blue eyes and dark hair." Haley's interest in my clothes always baffles me. Killers and murder plots are more my speed. "Wear your hair up. Like actually up, maybe a twist with curls hanging down to soften it."

I let Haley enjoy dressing me up over the phone, but

163

only half-listen. A fancy dinner party is way out of my usual. I'd rather stay home and snuggle with Lucas on the couch, but he promised his mom and I want to support him.

"I'll come up with something," I finally say after she's progressed from a simple twist to a complicated up-do that I don't understand.

"You have him on the hook now. You have to wow him."

"I'll wow him just fine, but thanks for the fashion advice. Get back to me as soon as you can on the coin thing, okay?"

"You got it. Have fun tonight."

The quiet of my car seems louder after listening to Haley, but I'm thankful for the friend. For some reason, she likes me. Besides her baffling interest in fashion, I like her too.

Minus living through Lucy's murder, today's been a pretty good day.

Now just to get through the party with Lucas' dad and creepy mom.

Chapter 20

Gabby

My curls refuse to be tamed into any semblance of an elegant up-do that Haley urged me to wear tonight. No matter how many times I twist it up and pin it, I look like some odd rabbit with dark curls for ears.

Chester watches me from his usual seat on the back of the toilet. "Don't stare at me like that. I know I look ridiculous." Chester only blinks.

Between the dress with too-short sleeves and my mess of an attempt at a fancy hair-do, I feel like an imposter. "You think Lucas would mind if I wore jeans?" I ask Chester, only half-joking.

He licks his paw and ignores my question.

Lucas knocks on my front door and my stomach clenches with excitement and apprehension at our first official date. I dart a last look in the mirror and hate my hair.

"Crap on a cracker." I pull out the many pins and shake my fingers through my curls. The wild mess surrounding my face looks like the reflection I'm used to. "Better," I tell Chester.

If Lucas feels self-conscious in his dark suit and bright blue tie, he doesn't show it. The suit fits his broad shoulders perfectly, the color of his tie highlights his eyes. The sight of him knocks the breath from my chest.

"You clean up good," I quip to cover my instant nerves, stepping back to let him into the house.

"So do you." He runs his eyes over my body and I'm conscious of all the places the fabric clings and the amount of skin showing. His eyes light last on my white dress gloves, but slide away. His eyes never narrow at the gloves, just accepts them as part of the package.

My heart skips faster at the acceptance.

I slide one arm into the best coat I own and he steps forward to help me. "Always the gentleman." A nervous giggle escapes my lips. I bite them to stop the sound.

He stares at my lower lip caught in my teeth. "Don't be nervous. This is just a party full of stuffy patrons to the museum, nothing to fear."

"Easy for you to say. These are your parents and their friends. You're used to them. I'm the town freak."

"Stop that." His harsh words bring me up short. "You are not a freak."

I've soured the mood. "Sorry, I'm just nervous."

"Don't be." He leans in suddenly and kisses me deeply, completely. All my nerves melt away. With his lips on mine, the entire world and my place in it snaps into focus. Nothing matters but this man.

He breaks the kiss and I stand with my eyes closed.

"Feel better?"

I open my eyes to his face close to mine, blink a few times. "Much better. Can you do that every time I get nervous?"

His husky voice fills my living room, "Any time you need it." He drops another quick kiss on my lips, then opens the door. "Let's go before I change my mind." His tone leaves no doubt about what he'd rather be doing with me than going to this party.

The anticipation fills me with wonder as well as fear. I open the door, my hand shaking on the knob. "After you," I say and hold the door for him.

He walks out ahead of me, his hand trailing across my hip as he passes. The cold night air blows against the skin of my bare legs, swirls under my skirt, but all I feel is the heat Lucas created.

On the drive to the antique car museum in Coburn, I want to tell him about Lucy being murdered, about my conversation with Dustin, about the coins and the newspaper clippings. Grandma's warning about living, not obsessing about cases, stills my tongue on the subject. This night is an island of happiness and time with Lucas. Tomorrow his sister will still be dead and a killer will still be on the loose. We can discuss it tomorrow.

Tonight is precious and doesn't need tainted by blood.

"How long has your mom been on the board at the museum?" I ask.

"Years now. Since we were in school. She loves classic cars. Has a collection of her own out in the barn behind our house."

"I didn't know that." I can't picture Deidre as a car buff.

"Anything fancy and high class is her style," Lucas responds. "She only has the best of the best. Cords, Duesenbergs, a bunch of other ones I don't know the names of. They're pretty amazing. Nothing like the cars we have now."

"Does your dad like cars too?"

"He likes making mom happy."

River Bend fades away as we drive down the country highway towards Coburn. I stare at the dark fields, thinking. "My dad liked old cars, too." I say.

"I forgot about that," Lucas says. "Didn't he work at the auction park or something?"

"He was a mechanic. He worked on all the cars that needed checked out before they went on the auction block." More fields and trees slide past my window. My mind slides into the past. "I haven't thought about that for a long time. I've been so focused on where he is now, I haven't let myself remember who he was before."

Lucas weighs his response carefully. "Where do you think he is now?"

"Out there, somewhere." I motion to the dark countryside.

I've soured the mood again. Determined to keep the evening light, I abruptly change the subject. "Will the food be good at the party?"

Lucas chuckles. "Are you hungry?"

"Always," I tease.

"The food's always good. The Kingston Winery does the catering."

"That's the people who catered my party. Mrs. Mott's nephew Lane and his wife Vee own it right?"

"Maybe. I just know they make a wonderful prime rib."

"And wine. Their wine is amazing. And I don't even drink much."

"Don't drink too much tonight," he warns.

"Why?" I try not to be offended. "I can drink if I want."

"I'd like you to have all your senses about you later." Another ripple of excitement shivers up my back at his sexy tone. In all the years I've known Lucas, this is a side of him I've never seen.

A side of him I greatly enjoy and want more of.

"Maybe just one glass." My voice sounds similarly husky and flirtatious. I barely recognize it.

He recognizes my meaning.

He reaches his hand to my cheek, runs the back of one finger down my delicate skin. "Just one," he repeats. I melt at the promise.

If Lucas actually kissed me every time my nerves got to me, we'd spend the entire night making out. Just walking in the door makes me quake. The other guests are decked out in lovely dresses and sharp suits. In my bathroom at home, I felt overdressed.

I feel shabby and worn in my sweater dress against the satiny fabric of the other women. My dress was purchased

169

by Grandma Dot with love and that has to count for more than money to burn on expensive clothes.

I cling to Lucas' hand for support, my palm growing sweaty inside my white gloves.

Deidre Hartley glides towards us through a break in the crowd. She's a vision in white drapes with fur edgings. She walks lightly on impossibly thin and tall heels, not a wobble in sight.

In my sensible flats, her loveliness towers over me, but doesn't reach her eyes. The expertly applied makeup can't cover the vacant look in her eyes or transform the forced smile into warmth.

"Lucas, my dear, so glad you made it," Deidre exclaims kissing Lucas on both cheeks. I have to stifle a laugh at her over-blown greeting. Lucas doesn't seem to notice anything out of the ordinary, so maybe Deidre's pretension is her usual demeanor. The woman before me bears little resemblance to Crystal's mom I remember from childhood. Maybe losing her daughter damaged her.

The thought makes me instantly contrite. This woman has been through more than I ever hope to endure. If she wants to be dramatic, let her.

"Nice to see you again, Mrs. Hartley," I say sweetly, even though she hasn't acknowledged my existence.

Her eyes flitter over me, a quick assessing look at my dress, her eyes lingering on my gloves. Her lips purse for a beat and she replies, "Gabby."

She quickly turns her attention back to Lucas, wrapping herself around his arm. "I have so many people who want to see you," she says brightly, steering Lucas away. He has no choice but to drop my hand and go with his mom. He looks over his shoulder and mouths, "Sorry."

"Deidre lives for showing him off," Gregor says suddenly near my elbow.

"I don't blame her," I say evenly fighting an absurd stab of jealousy.

"Would you like a drink?" he asks. "Holding something in your hands helps with nerves at a social function. Gives you something to do to expel the build-up of energy."

Heat rises on the back of my neck, remembering Lucas' comments earlier about drinking alcohol. "I'd love a soda."

Gregor leads me towards the bar in the corner and orders a Pepsi. It's served in a heavy glass. Even the drinks are better dressed than I am.

The carbonation in the soda tingles my nose as I take nervous sip after sip. "See," Gregor says, "Expels your nervous energy."

"Who says I'm nervous?" I try for casual confidence, but can't keep a straight face.

"I come to this dumb thing every year and I'm nervous. Rather be home walking Maverick or in my study."

"If you're not into all this, why do you do it?" I catch sight of Lucas across the room, talking to an older couple with his mom. He feels my eyes on him and turns to give me a smile across the room.

Gregor sees the interaction. "We do things we don't

want to do for those we love," he says, nodding to Lucas.

"Why does Deidre do it? I surprised she'd come this year, after…."

"She loves the cars, the people, the money around her. She has quite a collection of her own at home."

"Lucas was telling me about it on the way over here."

"She buys and sells cars at the auction. It's just a way to hob-nob with the bigwigs. A lot of famous people come to that car auction. It's world-famous. Buyers from all over the world purchase and sell there. The actual auction is really interesting. The psychology of buying at auction is fascinating to watch."

I take a large drink of my soda, prepared to listen to another lecture Gregor can't stop himself from giving. "Uh-huh," I grunt, scanning the crowd for Lucas again. Deidre's steered him away from the older couple and has him surrounded by three middle-aged men in flashy suits.

"New money," Gregor says following my line of sight and abandoning his dissertation on auction psychology. "Newcomers to the auction scene here. Deidre always pays the new ones close attention. Keeps them coming back."

Gregor means well, but I came here to spend time with Lucas, not make small talk with his dad. As I watch, Deidre flicks a look over her shoulder at me, her eyes narrowed and her smile almost genuine.

I see you.

"Excuse me," I say to Gregor, sitting my empty glass on the bar. "I'm going to claim my date."

Gregor chuckles. "You've got spunk, girl. I see why he

likes you so much."

I sail calmly through the crowd to Lucas. He sees me approaching and his smile brightens. "Gentlemen, this is Gabby McAllister, my date."

Shoving between Deidre and Lucas, I wrap myself around his arm the way she did earlier. "So nice to meet you," I say so politely, Grandma Dot would beam with pride. "Lucas, dear, could you come with me, please?" My tone sounds eerily similar to the one Deidre used earlier.

Lucas follows me easily. "Thanks for saving me," he whispers.

"That's just that psychic woman you've seen on the news," I overhear Deidre saying to the men.

I want to turn around and defend myself. I want to tell Lucas his mom's a phony and a flake. I want to drag him out of here and back to River Bend.

"Can we go look at the cars on display?" I ask instead. "This place is so beautiful. I'd love to look around before dinner."

"Beautiful and romantic," Lucas says. "Want to re-enact the car scene in Titanic?"

A genuine, full-hearted laugh tumbles out of me. "You're awful," I say pushing myself into his side as he leads me to the museum.

"That wasn't a no," he teases.

Chapter 21

Gabby

The cars at the museum are beautiful, but Lucas captures all my attention. Strolling hand in hand past the expensive vehicles, I listen to the deep timbre of Lucas' voice and the soft music playing overhead. Other guests admire the cars, drifting past the softly lit displays in their elegant attire.

If I squint, I can imagine we are somewhere exotic, not in small-town Indiana. But magic can happen anywhere, and the space between our bodies as we walk is bursting with magic.

The overhead tone announcing dinner breaks the spell.

A mixture of dread and sympathy fills me as we approach our table where Deidre holds court over Gregor and two other couples. I want to like this woman. She gave birth to the amazing man at my side. Lucas obviously dotes on her. I search her face as she entertains the other guests with some story and the guests laugh along. Maybe her smile isn't fake, maybe her over-the-top ways hide deep self-doubt.

Maybe she doesn't know how to act or who to be now

that she knows her daughter was murdered.

Sympathy wins over the dread and I greet her warmly as I take the seat Lucas pulls out for me. "Deidre, the cars in this museum are so amazing," I gush. "I can see why you're so interested in all this."

Deidre blinks at me twice, calculating a response. I keep a smile plastered to my face. I need this woman to like me.

"You're sweet," she says graciously and introduces me to the other couples. "This is Gabby McAllister and you all know my son, Lucas."

"Gabby is the woman who found our daughter," Gregor supplies.

An older gentleman opens his mouth to ask the inevitable questions. Deidre cuts him off. "Let's not talk about that tonight," she says firmly. "I love that dress," she says to me, the smallest barb lurking under the simple words.

I give her the response she craves, "Not nearly as lovely as yours. Where did you get it?"

"Yes, where did you find such an amazing concoction," one of the other women jumps into the conversation.

Lucas sneaks me a sideways glance and the barest of eye rolls as Deidre regales them with details of her shopping trip to Chicago. I relax into my seat and let their inane conversation fade into background noise.

By the time dessert is served on delicate china plates, I'm more than ready to leave the party. Polite small talk over linen table cloths and fancy place settings feels like a waste of time with Lucas so close and handsome.

His warm hand lands on my bare thigh, hidden under the table. "You look nervous again." He leans close to so only I can hear. "Do you need me to fix that?"

My lips begin to tingle at the suggestion. I push them together and lean closer to Lucas.

"That's an interesting tattoo," the same older gentleman that wanted to ask me about finding Crystal says suddenly.

I snap up straight in my chair like a child caught sneaking an extra dessert. On reflex, I cover the tattoo with my hand. Six pairs of eyes are focused on me now. Deidre's chair is empty. I'd been so intent on Lucas I hadn't noticed her departure.

"Thank you?" I try to keep the question out of the words, but fail.

"Does it signify anything?" Gregor asks. "Oftentimes, people get important symbols tattooed on themselves to commemorate events or beliefs."

If they only knew.

"Just the usual things a cross signifies," I reply vaguely.

To my horror, the tattoo begins to tingle. I ignore it, hoping it's just a reaction to the attention.

The first man flicks a quick look over his shoulder then asks, "How do you do what you do? How did you find...?" He snaps his mouth shut, realizing too late that Deidre may be gone, but Gregor and Lucas might not appreciate the question.

Below my hand, the tattoo burns.

177

Bathroom.

Not now, not now, I silently beg, pushing harder at the tattoo.

"Gabby just senses things," Lucas comes to my rescue. "She sees things when she touches them."

"What kinds of things?" one of the women asks. Everyone at the table leans closer, curious.

I can't focus on the question. One word pounds in my head.

Bathroom.

Deidre returns to the table, saving me from answering. "Took care of that," she exclaims as she retakes her seat. The man who started this line of questioning looks crushed at losing his opportunity.

"You can make an appointment at my shop and I can show you if you like," I say as politely as possible with the pain in my arm growing. I look desperately at Lucas, "I need to use the restroom," I manage to get out before grabbing my purse and fleeing the table.

"I'll do that," I hear the man call after me.

Bracing myself for what I will find in the bathroom, I pause at the swinging door and take a deep breath. "Lord let me do what you need me to do." I push on the door and it swings inward.

The bathroom is empty except for a red-head leaning on both hands against the granite counter. Her sniffling fills the expertly decorated room. Noticing my arrival, she stands up quickly and turns on the water.

I recognize her reflection. Vee Markle, the bartender from my party and the owner of the catering company at this event.

"Are you okay?" I ask gently.

"I'm fine," she lies, then busies herself with washing her hands and surreptitiously wiping tears from under her eyes. I hand her a paper towel to dry her face.

"You don't look fine."

Vee looks into the mirror and recognizes me. "Oh crap," she says under her breath. "Guess I can't fool you, of all people."

I don't know how to answer that, so I let her continue, watching her intently in the reflection.

"It's just his job." She waves her arm towards the door. "Lane loves doing this catering thing, but I hate it. These rich snobs suck."

Her childish manner makes me smile. "Did something happen?"

A faraway look crosses her face. "Just the usual. I should be used to it by now," she says cryptically.

"If you don't like catering, why do you do it?" I don't know what else to ask.

A bark of rueful laughter fills the room. "Why do you think? Money. Never enough of that." She balls up the paper towel and tosses it in the trash.

"Did you know Lucy Reed?"

Vee freezes, her arm still raised from throwing the paper towel.

"I heard you and some other people hung out a lot together in high school," I prompt.

"We did." She drops her arm. "In high school."

"Were you still close?"

179

She takes a step towards the door. "Not really."

I step closer. "Do you know she was murdered?"

Vee's face blanches and she makes a small sound of surprise. "She died in an accident," she protests.

"She was murdered." I step towards her again, watching her reactions intently. "Do you know anything about that?"

Surprise, confusion and fear flitter across her face. I'm looking for guilt, but fear wins out. "I don't know anything." She looks to the door, gauging the distance. "I have to go. Lane will need me."

"Do you collect coins, Vee?"

She ignores the question and rushes out of the bathroom.

The door swings back and forth a few times, then settles closed.

I use the restroom and wash my hands, replaying the encounter in my head, looking for something useful. Vee didn't really say anything.

"At least she's not crying right now," I say to my reflection. As I retrieve my gloves from my purse, I hear my phone vibrating. It's Haley. I answer, excited for news.

"I hate to bother you on your hot date, but I thought you'd want to hear what I found out," she says.

"You work fast," I say, impressed.

"You hired the best," she laughs. "How's the hot detective?"

"Your information?" I prod her back on track.

"Fine, keep all the juicy details to yourself. I have

some more digging to do, but so far, many of the coins you sent me info on are reported stolen. Some from that museum theft years ago, some others from various home invasions."

"That's what I figured." I rub stray dribbles of water off the granite countertop.

"What you didn't figure out was that a man in Spain was arrested several years ago, mostly white-collar stuff."

"Okay? I don't see the connection."

"When they raided his house, well more of a compound actually, but anyway, they found a bunch of these stolen coins at his house."

"The same coins Lucy had?"

"Yep. And this is why I'm interrupting your romantic interlude, this guy also had quite a car collection. Did you know there was a fancy car company in Auburn back in the early 1900's?"

"I'm at that museum right now," I point out. "I was just looking at some Auburns."

"Auburns are really rare cars and super expensive. This guy had several of them as well as a bunch of other cars."

I pause in my wiping of the counter. "An antique car collector in Spain? How did he get them?"

"That's the super-sleuthing part I had to do. He bought them at the auction where you are."

My mind reels with the information. "What does a guy in Spain have to do with Lucy and with Crystal for that matter?"

"I'm just the tech girl, you're the detective."

"I'm not a detective," I point out.

"Well, your boyfriend is."

The swinging door to the bathroom moves slightly, but remains closed. I stare at the door as I ask. "What's this guy in Spain's name?"

"Ferdinand Gomez. Sounds mysterious, doesn't it?"

"Ferdinand Gomez," I repeat. "All of this is mysterious."

"Never a dull moment with you, Gabby," Haley says happily. "Worry about all this later and enjoy your date."

I turn the water on and off, thinking. "I will. Thanks, Haley."

I return the phone to my purse and put my gloves back on. "Ferdinand Gomez, who are you?" I ask my reflection.

Distracted, I push the door open hard and run into Deidre. She jumps back, startled. I laugh nervously, "Sorry about that. I wasn't paying attention."

"No worries, dear," she replies. "Are you having a nice time tonight?"

A quick glance down the hall confirms we are alone. "Deidre, can I ask you a serious question?"

The forced smile returns to her face, "You can ask me anything."

"Are you upset I'm dating Lucas?"

My honesty shakes her, but she composes herself quickly. "I love my son," she says simply.

"But are you upset about me?" I push.

"You make him happy."

She hasn't answered my question, but I accept the small olive branch. "He makes me very happy, too."

For her, the matter is settled, and she pushes past me to the bathroom door, the flowing white drapes of her dress trailing behind her.

The circle of eager faces at the table watch me return. Lucas stands to pull out my chair. I don't sit down, but lean close and ask. "Would it be rude to leave now?"

Lucas looks around the room, "Dinner's over and they're just finishing up with the silent auction items. I suppose we can sneak out."

I soften my request with a flirty, "I haven't had any wine at all."

My suggestion lights his desire to get me home and he readily agrees.

After a few departure pleasantries to the table, Lucas intercepts Deidre and says his good-byes. I wait politely nearby, anxious to escape.

We finally leave the museum and step out into the cold night. The sky above is clear, the stars glittering like cold diamonds in the black. The magic returns to the space between our sides as we hurry to his car.

He opens my door for me and I climb in, the leather upholstery cold against the backs of my bare legs.

"You didn't seem to get too nervous," he says. "I never got the change to kiss your nerves away."

"I'm a little nervous now," I tease.

He takes the bait and leans to me, only brushes his lips against mine in a promise of more to come.

"Will you take me home?" I ask breathlessly.

He eagerly agrees and starts the engine. The magic fills the entire inside of his car as I lean my head against his shoulder. We drive home wordlessly, his hand possessively on my thigh, his fingers pressing against my flesh.

Chapter 22

Lucas

The chill on Gabby's bare skin quickly fades as I caress her thigh on the drive home. She leans her head against my shoulder and her curls tickle my cheek. I want to stay like this forever with her, but am also eager for the promise of more once we reach her house.

"You handled tonight very well," I say. "I know my mom can be a bit much. Especially in the last few days."

She moans um-uh and tucks closer against me.

"My dad can go on and on. He forgets we're not all psychology students." I don't know why I feel the need to apologize for my parents, Gabby apparently didn't mind their eccentricities. Her snuggled pose proves she forgives me for them.

"Stop talking," she says. "Just enjoy this night."

I follow her advice, slide my hand an inch higher on her thigh, and push harder on the gas pedal.

On the front step of her house, she fiddles with the keys at the lock. The keys hit the concrete step with a rattle.

"Crap on a cracker." Bending over to retrieve the keys, she provides me with a nice view of her bottom, the back of her dress riding high.

"I really like that dress," I say suggestively.

She stands and faces me with the keys in her hand. "You just want to take it off me." There's a question in her eyes.

I kiss her fully in answer, then take the keys from her hand. The key slides in easily, and I turn the lock and open the door.

We leave the lights turned off inside the house. Our lips find each other as our hands pull off coats and we kick off shoes. I've lied to myself for a long time about my feelings for Gabby. Tonight I will show her the truth, nothing else matters.

Through my haze of desire, I hear the meow of a cat. Gabby laughs suddenly against my mouth.

"Chester, you're interrupting," she says pulling away from me to pick up the cat. "Let me put him in the bathroom so he doesn't bother us."

I watch her walk down the short hall in the dark, enjoying every curve of her body in the dim light. I run a hand over my hair and take a deep breath to steady myself.

After shutting the door on the cat, she reaches her hand for me, "Where were we?" she asks suggestively. I take her gloved hand in mine and let her lead me down the hall to her room.

I pull off my suit jacket and tie and drop them on a chair already piled high with clothes. Desire and nerves pound through my blood as I draw close to where she stands in the moonlight.

I take one of her hands in mine and pull the glove off. "You won't need these tonight." I remove the other glove and toss them both towards the chair of clothes.

She reaches tentative hands to my face, then smoothes my cheeks. "Nothing," she murmurs. "Just your skin." Free to touch with her bare hands, she explores all the skin she can find, even slipping her hands into my shirt and down my chest.

Her fingertips drive me wild and I struggle to contain my reaction. *Make it last, make it last.*

I grab the hem of her dress and pull it slowly over her head. She wriggles her hips to help me remove the dress, further driving me wild.

Her body dressed only in bra and panties is beyond beautiful in the moonlight. I stand back to get a full view of her skin. Blood pounds through my body at the sight, my chest aches from the glory of her.

I kiss her neck and she groans. My lips trail down her shoulder, my hands slide down her arms. I lift her arm and place a kiss on her tattoo.

She stiffens.

Shocked, I pull back. "What's wrong?"

She pulls her arm from my grasp and covers her chest. "I need to tell you something before we do this."

The desire that nearly consumed me a moment ago fizzles away. We need to talk, can never be good. Fighting an edge of panic at whatever can be so important that she chose now to tell me, I sit on the bed. She sits

187

next to me, pulling a blanket around her shoulders.

"Earlier tonight, that man asked about my tattoo?"

"Right." I try to be patient.

"Your dad asked if it signified something."

I'm beginning to lose patience at the conversation. "I was there, I remember."

"This is more than a tattoo. Yes, I love God and I'm proud to show it, but there's more to it."

She pauses to gather her thoughts. I wait for her to continue.

"I get messages from God from my tattoo," she says quickly. "Tonight at dinner when I left so fast to go to the bathroom? My tattoo was tingling and I kept hearing 'bathroom' in my head. When I went I found a woman who was upset and I talked to her." Her words practically fall on top of each other in her hurry to get them out. "Things like that happen all the time. My tattoo will burn or tingle and I hear commands in my head. I always obey them. I need to help people or find something or whatever God needs me to do. I always do what God needs me to do, even if I look foolish or rude like tonight."

She looks at me in the moonlight, her eyes pleading for me to understand.

"Why do you need to tell me this now?"

"I need you to understand who I am, all of who I am, before…." She motions to the bed.

"Were you afraid I'd run away scared of you or something?" I touch her bare hand next to mine to show her I'm teasing.

"Something like that," she hedges. "It's happened
188

before."

I'd always wondered why she and Preston broke up so abruptly, but never asked. "He's an idiot," I say.

"So you're not freaked out?" The hope and longing in her face is endearing.

I take her face in both my hands, lock my eyes with hers. "Nothing you've ever done has freaked me out. It's a little strange, but it's just who you are. And I love you for it."

We both flinch. I hadn't intended to tell her I loved her. The romantic part of our relationship is so new, I hadn't even thought about it.

"You love me?" she asks quietly.

I don't hesitate. "I love you, Gabby. I think I've always loved you."

"Show me," she says, her fingers tugging at the buttons on my shirt.

The desire I felt for this woman a few minutes ago is pale compared to what I feel for her now. We tear at our clothes and toss them on the floor. Fully exposed and laying on the bed, her beauty consumes me. "I love you, Gabby," I say again.

"I love you too, Lucas." Her words melt any vestige of control I had. She pulls me to her and my body covers hers.

Nothing in my life compares to this moment.

Nothing in my life will be the same after.

Chapter 23

Gabby

Languid, luxurious, liquid, and sweet. Innumerable descriptions for the night I just spent with Lucas. I roll over in bed and slip my arm over his bare chest. His skin, hot from sleeping, presses against mine.

One word describes this moment.

Precious.

I trail my hand across his chest hair and he moans softly.

Absolutely precious.

I watch him sleep as the morning sun transforms the room from shadow to brightness. I feel similarly transformed. I opened my self to this man and he accepted me completely.

He rolls towards me and wraps his arms around me. I wriggle into a more comfortable position, forming my body to his. My mind drifts to all the reasons I am blessed. All the things I have to be thankful for.

"Thank you, Lord, for this man," I whisper as I drift back to sleep.

When I wake again, Lucas isn't in the bed with me. For a panicked moment, I think maybe the previous night had been a dream.

I smell coffee and hear the TV from down the hall and the panic disappears.

After pulling on soft pants and an old sweater, I use the restroom and wash my face. My current reflection is a far cry from last night's fancy attire. I hope Lucas doesn't mind.

I find him on the couch watching the morning news. He's wearing his dress pants and undershirt, one foot propped up on the coffee table.

"You looked so precious sleeping, I didn't want to wake you," he says. He said 'precious' and I love him even more for it.

"Guess you wore me out," I tease.

"There's coffee. I hope it's okay I helped myself."

I pour myself a cup and catch myself before I drink it too soon and burn my tongue. "Help yourself to whatever you need," I say, joining him on the couch, sitting so close our legs touch. Chester sits next to me, begging for attention.

The morning is perfect until Lacey Aniston fills the TV with a story. She explains how Lucy's death has been ruled a homicide and adds a veiled accusation about Lucy and Crystal being connected and how I am involved in both cases.

Irritated with what once again Lacey pretends is news, I change the channel.

Anger radiates off of Lucas.

"Don't worry about her. She just hates me," I try to soothe.

"You didn't tell me Lucy was murdered or that it was connected to Crystal." The anger I thought was directed at Lacey is actually at me.

"I didn't want to ruin last night," I say meekly.

"You should have told me." He moves a little away on the couch, far enough so our legs no longer touch.

"You're right. I should have told you. I was going to tell you this morning." I sit my coffee on the table. "I wasn't hiding it from you. There's lots of things I need to talk to you about."

His body is still stiff, but he says, "I'm listening."

"Grandma Dot was doing Lucy's hair to prepare for her funeral," I begin. As I tell him everything that happened and everything I learned, his body slowly relaxes. The anger melts into curiosity. I finish my story with what Haley told me about the man in Spain with similar stolen coins.

"I didn't want to bring it up last night. I had other things on my mind." I hope my flirty tease will break the final tension between us.

Lucas considers all I said and finally agrees with me. "Better things," he says and slides back across the couch so we are touching again.

Relief floods me. I certainly didn't want to fight with him so soon after what we shared.

"Does Dustin know about all this?" Lucas asks, absently trailing a finger up and down my arm.

"Not all of it. Haley just told me last night."

"Write down everything she said." He stands up and takes his cup to the kitchen. "I'll take it to the station and share it with Dustin and see what else we can find out."

"I thought you weren't allowed to work on the case."

"I'd like to see him try and stop me. If my sister was murdered because of some stolen coins, I will find out."

Crossing the living room, I reach up for a quick kiss, "You're sexy when you're determined."

"You're sexy all the time," he replies. "Write that stuff down, okay?"

Lucas goes to retrieve his clothes and I find a pad and paper. I'd rather spend a relaxing morning with him. "Better get used to being with a cop," I tell Chester.

As I finish writing what Haley told me, Lucas returns to the kitchen. His tie and jacket thrown over his arm and his half-buttoned dress shirt giving me a nice view of his chest. He slips into his shoes, his mind already out the door and on the case.

"You're not mad I have to go?" he asks as he slides into his coat.

"Not at all," I say honestly. "I have a few clients today anyway."

The relief on his face is endearing. He drops a quick kiss on my lips. I want to cling to him, but let him go.

"I picked up an extra patrol shift tonight, but can I come by after?" His eyes sparkle with naughty mischief.

"You better," I tease back.

The front door barely shuts behind him when he yells for me. "Gabby, come out here." The anger and fear in his voice bring me running into the cold.

He stands in the driveway, pointing at my crooked garage door.

MURDERER is scrawled across the peeling paint in stark block letters.

"Holy crap, not again." I shudder against the cold and the hatred in the writing.

Lucas boils with anger, his fists clenched at his sides. "Again?"

"I get vandalized a lot." I swallow to keep my voice steady.

Don't let it shake you. That's what they want.

He paces in front of the vulgar word, runs his hand through his hair again and again. "I was right inside. I could have caught them."

His anger surprises me. "It's nothing. Really, I'm used to it."

He spins on his heel and barks, "You shouldn't have to get used to it. How could someone think you had anything to do with Lucy and Crystal?" His sister's name comes out in a strange strangled sound.

"Lacey basically said as much on her news report," I point out.

"I'm going to…"

I cut him off. "You're going to go to work and catch the actual killer. I'm going to clean off this paint and go to meet my clients. These jerks just want to upset me. I don't let them." My hands shake with anger, but I don't tell him that.

He turns his back on the garage door and blows air in

exasperation. "You're shivering," he says suddenly and rubs his hands up and down my arms. "Go inside. I'll try to come by later and paint over it."

"I have paint remover," I protest.

"I want to do this for you. Please, let me."

The offer is so sweet, I agree and wave to him as he drives away.

Alone in the freezing driveway, I look at the awful word. My bare feet burn from the cold concrete and the wind whips through my thin sweater. I begin to shake all over.

After all the good I've done in this town, many still believe the worst of me. I told Lucas it was no big deal, but it's a personal slap in the face.

I grab a rock and scratch furiously at the letters. Deep gauges mar the door, remnants of past vandals show faintly despite the many times I've used the paint remover. Desperate to remove the stains, I scratch until an emptiness replaces the hurt anger.

Panting, with scuffed knuckles, I throw the rock at the door. It leaves a dent then rolls to the side of the driveway.

I can still read the word, but it's lost the ability to hurt me.

Chapter 24

Dustin

A full day of following up on the information Gabby gave us this morning hasn't provided many useful leads. I'd love to talk to Ferdinand Gomez in Spain and find out how he acquired the stolen coins found in his home. Even if a small-town cop from Indiana was able to question him, I'd be out of luck.

Ferdinand Gomez was killed in prison not long after he was arrested. I found that little nugget today. It fills me with a petty sense of victory over Gabby's amateur hacker. One point to me.

I shift in the driver's seat of my cruiser, ashamed of myself. Solving a case is not a competition. But man, it feels good to win one for a change.

The only lead I have left to check out is the connection between Lane and Vee Markle to both Crystal and Lucy. Childhood friends of the victims is a flimsy connection, but it's all I have to go on at the moment. Maybe they'll remember something about Crystal's disappearance.

Acres of vineyard stretch alongside Kingston Road, the

spindly vines sad in the moonlight as they wait for spring to perk them back into life. As the vineyards continue, I'm amazed at the amount of land the Markles own. Lane and Vee were a few years younger than me in school, but I remember them as the burn out type. Their social lives were a far cry from my structured sports practices and Friday night basketball games. They've overcome their slow start in life to amass such land as this.

Their mysterious rise to wealth as well as Lucy's sets my gut quaking. There might be more of a connection than just childhood friends. I have no idea what it could be, but I'm anxious to find out.

Lane and Vee's house sits nestled among the acres of withered vines. A large processing plant squats dark nearby. The Kingston Winery and Catering sign illuminated by a floodlight. The lighted sign is the only bright spot on the property. Every window on the plant and the house is dark.

I radio in to give my location. "Looks like no one's home, but I'm going to knock anyway," I tell dispatch. My breathe puffs in small clouds against the cold as I walk up the sidewalk. I'm alone on the property, but my senses are on high alert just the same. Suddenly wishing I'd brought Lucas or someone else with me, I stop on the walk. I listen to the night, sniff the air, scan the far corners of the property.

My senses tell me nothing, but I feel it. There's something wrong here.

I turn on my body-cam and unsnap my holster. The windows of the house stare blankly at me, the curtains perfectly still.

Go back, get out.

I listen to my gut and take one step towards my cruiser. "Wonder if this is how Gabby gets messages," flitters through my mind.

A gunshot echoes through the darkness.

I brace for the pain, but it doesn't come. The shot came from inside the house, not directed to me.

"Shots fired," I bark into my radio. "Kingston Winery. Shots fired."

I'm halfway up the front stairs before I finish the radio transmission, my gun in hand.

The front door is closed, but the handle turns easily. The door swings inward, a dark gaping hole into more darkness. With my back to the door jamb, I listen for any sounds inside the house.

Over the pounding of blood in my ears, I hear a woman pleading from the second story, "Please, please. We didn't tell anyone. I swear we didn't. We wouldn't."

"You should have stuck to our agreement." The voice is eerily calm, and eerily familiar.

"You're right. I shouldn't have asked for more. Please don't."

Her begging is cut short by another gunshot from upstairs.

I flinch at the sound, sick to be so close but not fast enough to save Vee Markle.

Adrenaline pumps through my body, every inch of me tight with anticipation. I flex and release my muscles to loosen them, steady my breathing to calm my swirling mind.

With gun drawn and ready, I slide around the door jamb.

The scent of gun powder hangs heavy in the house. I shuffle through the dark in the direction I hope leads to the stairs. The shooter will have to come down them and I intend to be ready. A hall stretches from the front door to a glass patio door at the back of the house. The moonlight from the door outlines what looks like the bottom of a banister.

Sliding my heavy boots along the tile floor to silence my footsteps, I slink down the hall to the stairs, the weight of my gun in my hand reassuring.

The outline of a man merges with the banister, then stands silhouetted in the moonlight from the sliding door.

"Police," I shout as I turn on my flashlight.

The shout and the sudden light startle the figure and he spins to face me. In the beam of my flashlight, I can see his gun clearly.

"Drop the gun. Drop the gun," I shout, fighting adrenaline.

The man doesn't drop the gun. "You don't want to do this, Dustin," he says.

The face in the beam of my flashlight is familiar. I recognize the voice, the way he says my name.

"Dad? What the hell?" My hand shakes so badly, the circle of flashlight bounces off his face and around his body.

"Just back away and leave, son." Nathan McAllister says calmly. "This has nothing to do with you."

"You shot Lane and Vee, this has everything to do with me." The flashlight beam stops bouncing and I focus it on his face. The eyes I used to know, the eyes so similar to mine, stare directly into the beam. The warmth I remember seeing there is replaced with cold calculation. "Where have you been? How are you here?" I sound like a scared boy, eager for his father. I struggle for professional calm, reach for the emotional detachment I learned at academy.

They don't prepare you for this situation in academy.

He takes a step towards me, his gun trained on me as my gun's pointed at him. "This isn't the place for this conversation." His calm grates my frayed nerves.

"Fourteen years ago would have been a good time for this conversation." My mind reels to make connections, looks for a way this makes sense. It finds nothing. "All the blood in our kitchen when you were killed? I don't understand."

He shrugs, "We did a good job, didn't we?" He's so smug, my stomach turns.

"But mom?" My shock and confusion morph into anger. "You let her sit in prison all this time?" My voice high and strained. The sick feeling in my stomach grows. I never believed mom when she said she didn't kill him. I'd cut her out of my life completely. I'd deserted her.

She was innocent.

Saliva floods my mouth, a precursor to vomiting.

Keep it together.

"Business decisions can be hard," he replies with the same sickly-smug expression. "You have a decision to

201

make right now. Forget you ever saw me and leave or I can fix this another way." He takes another step towards me.

I want to run from him, want to run from the pain and betrayal from a man I've spent my whole life idolizing.

I press my heels into the tile floor and hold my ground.

"Drop the gun and put your hands behind your back," I say desperately. He takes another step, less than ten feet away from me now. "Drop the gun, damn it," I plead, my finger on the trigger.

He keeps his gun pointed at me, "I really don't want to do this," he says. "Last chance."

I hold my position, but the light beam begins swaying wildly from my shaking hands

"I warned you," he says then springs forward.

His shot rings in my ears and I pull my trigger in response.

Pain engulfs my shoulder. The impact spins me sideways, throws me into the wall. Shock and terror cause my legs to buckle. I slide down the wall, grappling for my gun that has tumbled from my now numb fingers.

He kicks the gun down the hall and it skitters across the tile. I try to reach for it, but only manage to lay full out on the floor.

He stands over me, grasping his arm. Blood oozes between his fingers and drips on my chest.

I'm sickly satisfied to see the blood, but I only grazed him.

No points to me for that mistake.

I lay on my back, gasping for air against the heavy

protective vest that offered no protection to my shoulder.

He drops to his knees and holds the gun against my temple. The hot mouth of the barrel singes against my skin. I flinch away from the heat.

"Stupid boy, I didn't want to shoot you," he growls. "Now we have a mess to clean up."

That calm, detached voice singes my heart.

"Why did you do it?" I gasp for answers. "We thought you were dead."

"You're sister didn't."

Through my terror and pain, I fear for Gabby. "Leave her alone," I try to scream. It comes out as a hoarse gurgle. A detached part of my mind wonders why I can't scream, why I can't talk.

"I don't want to hurt her. I want her to join us. We can use someone with her special skills."

An overwhelming need to cough overcomes me.

Hit my lung. Good God, this is bad.

I gag up phlegm and blood and spit it in his face.

He wipes it off his face and onto my chest. "That wasn't nice," he hisses. "I didn't have to hit your shoulder, you know. I could easily have got you in the head."

I moan in pain and betrayal. I've spent years missing the man I thought was my father. This monster only resembles the man I knew by his eyes. Everything else about him is a stranger.

"Promise not to get in my way, and I'll do you a favor," he says suddenly.

I don't want anything from this man except justice for

my family.

With the gun pressed to my head, I'm in no position to argue.

"I promise," I manage to croak. My chest aching with the effort.

"We have a deal coming up and it won't do for you to be snooping around. Be a good boy and mind your own business. Can you do that?"

A spasm of coughing won't let me speak, so I nod.

"That's my smart boy." He pushes the gun tight against my skull, then removes it. He fumbles on my chest until he finds my radio. "Officer down. Kingston Winery. Officer down."

He drops the radio back on my chest, stands, and kicks my gun further down the hallway.

"You never knew it, but I was at all your basketball games," he says, the moonlight from the sliding door behind him. "You were a talented kid and grew into an amazing man. I was even at your graduation from academy."

Words I would have died to hear before. Now I might die hearing them.

But he keeps talking and ruins it. "That Alexis is amazing, her and baby Walker. It would be a pity if something happened to them."

Stark terror courses through me, "Stay away from them," I choke out against another build-up of blood in my throat.

He doesn't answer. He's disappeared out the sliding door and into the night.

I lay in the silent house, my blood soaking my shirt and spreading on the tile beneath me. I strain to hear anything from upstairs. A cry in the dark, a shuffle of movement to let me know Vee and Lane might still be alive.

For several minutes, only my rasping breath and the occasional crackle of my radio fills the silent hall.

I focus on the radio transmissions from my fellow officers. Their many voices comfort me as my blood spreads on the tile, seeps into the waist of my pants.

Too much blood, too much blood.

Dad is alive and he shot me.

One voice crackles louder than the others.

"Dustin, if you can hear me, hold on." Lucas. My best friend in the world. I don't have the strength to reach the radio to respond.

Lucas is on the way.

I'll hold on for him.

I need to see Alexis again, need to pull her close to me at night in bed.

I'll hold on for her.

I need Walker. I must see him grow up. I must be the father I never had.

I'll hold on for him.

The darkness of the hall grows more complete and it gets harder to keep my eyes open. The safety vest pushes against my chest, each breath a battle.

I'll hold on. I'll hold on.

The hall fills with red and blue lights. I barely register their swirling pattern against the walls. The whooshing of my blood in my ears blocks out the sirens.

Voices shout to me as my fellows storm the house.

They're here.

I held on.

Chapter 25

Lucas

The acres of stretching vineyards can't pass quickly enough as I speed down the back road to Kingston Winery. My hands shake on the steering wheel and my eyes fuzz. I wipe the moisture away with impatient strikes at my eyes. *Let him be okay. Let him be okay.*

Overwhelming guilt swamps me. I should have been with him. He's my partner, my friend.

I wanted to make a little extra money to send to Olivia, so I picked up the extra patrol shift. Thinking of my young daughter increases my agitation. I want to call and hear her sweet voice, want to assure myself she's okay.

"Get your crap together, man," I yell in the car. "She's fine. Everyone's fine."

Except for Dustin.

He should have been fine.

I should have been with him.

I did deep for calm detachment as the house looms, the lights in the sky growing larger as I push on the gas pedal.

Gravel from the driveway skids from my tires as I slam

on the brakes next to the two cruisers that arrived before me. The pounding of my feet matches the pounding in my heart as I run to the house.

Let him be okay. Let him be okay.

Officer Patterson kneels next to Dustin's still body, pressing on his shoulder. The tile floor jams painfully into my knees as I land next to him.

"He's still alive?" I ask.

"Barely. The ambulance will be here any minute," Patterson says, his face pale and his eyes wide.

Patterson joined the force last summer and this is his first shooting victim.

"Keep the pressure on," I say gently. "Any other injuries you can see?" I scan Dustin's body, avoiding his face to keep my composure. The pool of blood surrounding the uniform is jarring enough.

"Looks like the blood's all from here, but I didn't want to move him until the medics arrive," Patterson answers.

"Less than an inch from his vest," I muse. "Luck or talent?"

I swim in helplessness, watch Dustin's chest rise and fall with labored breaths.

Keep breathing. Just keep breathing.

Activity from upstairs draws my attention from the tiny circle of Dustin, Patterson, and I. "What happened?"

"Two victims upstairs," Patterson tells me. "The homeowners, shot in the bedroom. Lane and Vee Markle. McAllister must have startled the shooter and got hit himself."

Holding Dustin's rough hand, I run the radio

transmissions through my mind. "Dustin called shots fired. Then a few minutes later, officer down." Something niggles at my mind. "Did you know Dustin well?"

"Not really," Patterson says.

"Well enough to recognize his voice on the radio, though, right?" I look at Dustin's face, thinking how much I want to hear that voice right now.

Another officer shouts into the house, "Ambulance is here."

"Did the officer down transmission sound like Dustin to you?" I ask Patterson.

Patterson has his eyes locked on the doorway, waiting anxiously for the medics. "I didn't pay much attention. Maybe it was a different voice," he says vaguely.

The rattle of a gurney being lowered from the ambulance and directions being called out almost drowns out the rattling word from Dustin.

I lean forward, my ear nearly touching his lips. "Dad," Dustin says.

Dropping his hand, I back into the front room, allow the medics to do their work in the hall.

I want to scream to the medics, "You have to save him, he's one of ours."

I don't have to say it out loud, each one of us is already thinking it. All the officers on-scene gather on the front lawn as the medics wheel Dustin out of the house. As a solid group, we watch in solemn silence as our fellow is loaded.

Lights and sirens flare into life and the ambulance speeds away. We watch until it turns onto the road.

Someone breaks the silence with a shout of, "Good luck, McAllister."

Our group breaks ups. A few men pat me on the shoulder with words of encouragement. "He's tough, he'll make it," and "We'll get this bastard," float around the front yard.

"He said it was his dad," I mumble to one of my friends in blue.

"His dead dad? He must be hallucinating."

"Maybe," I reply vaguely. "Maybe not." If Nathan McAllister shot his own son, what else might he do before I catch him?

How do I catch a ghost?

Chapter 26

Alexis

Walker crawls to the open tub of Christmas decorations and pulls to his chubby legs. My heart swells with pride at the accomplishment.

"Good job, buddy," I tell my son. "Won't Daddy be surprised to see you do that when he gets home."

Walker reaches into the tub and grabs a fragile glass ornament. I quickly put the lid on the tub and distract him with his favorite cop car toy. "You have to wait," I tell him.

We both have to wait. Dustin was going to be home earlier so we could decorate the tree together. "Just have to make a quick stop and follow up on something," he'd said.

I fight my usual battle with impatience. Dustin's quick stops usually take longer than he expects. In our four years of marriage, I've come to terms with his erratic schedule and unexpected calls away from us. I knew what I was getting into when I took my vows, and decided sharing Dustin with his job was better than not having him at all.

The empty tree bothers me tonight. The dark branches, bare of lights and glittering ornaments looks sad and lonely.

I feel sad and lonely.

Flipping through Facebook on my phone fills the emptiness for a while. Several friends have posted pictures of their decorations already. I imagine the pictures I can post tomorrow.

The phone rings in my hand and Lucas' number replaces Facebook on the screen.

Dread sinks into every inch of my body. Decoration pictures fade into meaningless nonsense.

I look at my son playing on the floor as the phone continues to ring, praying this call isn't going to change his life.

Lucas never calls me, has never had a reason to call me.

My mind fills with terror at what he might say.

I push the icon to answer, "Hello?"

Please, please, please.

"Alexis?"

His worried tone makes me want to scream and throw the phone.

My eyes locked on Walker, I ask, "He's hurt, isn't he?"

Lucas gets right to the point. "He's alive, but he's been shot."

The scream inside me claws to be let out. I don't want to scare Walker. I cling to the first part.

"He's alive?"

"They just took him in the ambulance. Alexis, I'm so sorry. He was shot in the shoulder, but it looks like the bullet may have nicked a lung." He stops talking suddenly, no doubt wanting to spare me the details.

I'm flying down the hall to our room, stepping out of my bright holiday pajama pants as I go. "But he's breathing? He's still with us?"

I need to hear it again. I need to hold to that fact.

"Yes." One word, full of sorrow and regret.

That's all I need to hear. I hang up on Lucas and drop the phone on our bed. The bed I sleep in with Dustin. The bed we made Walker in. The bed he will return to.

Any other option is unthinkable. Dustin is the strongest man I know. He'll fight with everything in him to return to us.

I pull on the first clothes I find and tuck my phone into my pocket.

The scream still claws at my throat.

I shut the bedroom door and shove my face into a pillow. It smells like Dustin.

The scream finds its release.

I give into the terror, to the pain, to the primal need to wail, until my throat hurts and my face burns. When I'm done, I hold Dustin's pillow to my chest, breathe in his scent for several moments.

Spent and empty, I drag myself from our bed and wash my face in our bathroom. Dustin's razor sits near the sink. I finger it, praying he'll use it again.

The initial rush of pain over, I jump into action.

I need to be near him.

As quickly as possible, I strap Walker into his carrier and toss a few things into his diaper bag. He still holds his cop car in his hand.

Right now, I hate the sight of it. Being a cop got his daddy shot.

I take the car from him and throw it across the kitchen. It hits the hard floor and a tire flies off.

Walker wails.

No matter how hard I try to stop them, tears stream down my cheeks.

Walker wails louder, sensing my upset.

Guiltily, I pick up the car with a missing tire and hand it back. "Sorry, buddy," I tell him, kissing his damp cheeks. "So sorry, buddy."

My tears stream unchecked as I swing the carrier over my arm and head to the door. I turn to grab my keys and see the empty Christmas tree in the living room.

"We'll be back," I tell the tree as I shut the door. "All three of us."

Chapter 27

Gabby

My mind spins as fast as the tires on my Charger as I drive towards the hospital. The call from Lucas and my call to Grandma Dot has me reeling. The heart-break in both their voices echoes my own emotions.

Lucas told me Dustin said, "Dad."

That breaks me more than anything. Dad must truly be alive.

And he shot Dustin.

Rage narrows my vision to slits of determination.

I make a u-turn and drive out of town towards Kingston Winery.

If I have any hope of finding Nathan McAllister, I need to see the scene.

There are so many vehicles at the winery, I have to park near the road. I hug the shadows as best I can and slink towards the house. If I can get close enough, I might be able to sneak into the scene.

From the far corner of the house, I duck under the yellow tape. Keeping to the bushes, I make my way towards the front porch. Several uniformed officers mill around, their backs to me.

Thankfully, none of them are Lucas.

A few feet from the front door, I straighten my back and raise my chin.

Pretend you have every right to be here and maybe no one will question you.

With fake confidence, I step out of the bushes and stride up the steps. I bump into an officer leaving the house, but look him in the eye and keep walking.

He lets me pass.

The pool of drying blood in the hall stops me cold.

Dustin's blood.

My chin quivers and I clench my teeth to stop it, transfixed by the blood.

"Gabby, what the crap?" Lucas exclaims, grabbing me by the arm and dragging me into the dining room away from everyone else.

"You're hurting me," I protest, prying his fingers off my arm.

He removes his hand and runs it over his head. "What are you doing here? You should be at the hospital."

"I can't help from the hospital. I need to be here, to see."

He visibly struggles for patience. "I know you want to help, but you can't just show up at a crime scene."

"Let me walk around for a few minutes. I won't touch anything. Well, I'll need to touch some things, but I won't mess up the scene. I promise."

He pushes both his hands against his eyes. "You're

putting me into a bad position here."

"Hartley," a loud voice booms from the next room.

"Crap, that's Chief Simmons." Lucas gives me a desperate look.

"Let me handle this." I spin on my heel and stride out of the dining room before Lucas can stop me.

"Hartley," Simmons bellows again. "Anyone see Hartley?"

I follow the bellow, then standing as tall as I can, I shove out a hand towards Simmons. "Chief Simmons, I'm Gabby McAllister. Sister of Detective McAllister." I give a small nod to the blood on the floor.

Lucas groans behind me as Simmons' wide face hardens. "What's she doing here?" he barks at Lucas, ignoring my outstretched hand.

"I'm here to help with this investigation. I'm sure you're familiar with my work on previous cases."

I push my gloved hand towards him again. Simmons stares at it, but won't touch me. "Is this some kind of joke?" he asks Lucas.

"No, sir," Lucas says contritely. A few officers have stopped to watch us now.

"I came on my own accord, Chief. Detective Hartley had nothing to do with it." I offer my hand one more time, testing him.

"She shouldn't be here," Simmons says, taking a step away from me.

"Since you won't touch my hand, you obviously believe I can do what I say I can," I say smugly.

A snicker rises from one of the on-looking officers and

adds to my confidence.

"Just let me look around a little bit and I'll get out of your way," I push.

Simmons considers, knowing I backed him into a corner. "You have five minutes," she snaps at me. "Hartley, come with me. Patterson, follow her."

Lucas follows Simmons outside without another look in my direction. A young man joins me. "I've heard about you," he says conspiratorially. "Pretty cool stuff you do."

"Thanks," I say shakily, nervous now that the confrontation is over. "This is where Dustin was shot?" I ask to have something to say.

"I found him right here," Patterson says.

"You found him?"

"I was first on the scene." He rubs his hands on his thighs. "McAllister was unconscious. I only found the one gun-shot to his shoulder. It was pretty bad." He darts his eyes for my reaction. "I'm sorry about your brother."

Panic for Dustin's safety rears inside me. Squeezing my eyes shut, I let Patterson lead me past the blood. "Can you show me where the other two victims were shot?"

"Upstairs. The coroner has already taken the bodies."

I follow Patterson up the steps to the master bedroom, my feet dragging on the steps. I hover outside the doorway, watch the forensic techs doing their work. Patterson stops near the bed and looks at me in the hall.

"You okay?"

I nod slowly and step into the room. The techs look up, curious. "Can I be alone here a minute?" I ask.

The techs look to Patterson. "Can we have the room?"

218

he asks.

A few grumbles and questioning looks, but the techs leave us.

"The male was shot in the bathroom," Patterson says. "Looks like he was coming out of the shower."

I enter the spacious bathroom, see the blood spatter on the shower curtain. I search for the bravado I used to confront Simmons and slide off my left glove.

"Can you stand outside the door?" I ask.

Patterson steps out but watches with interest.

I reach my bare hand to the stained shower curtain, braced for what I'll see.

The fabric of the curtain sends me nothing.

"Lord let me see what I need to see," I pray quietly and touch the actual blood.

The blood sends me nothing.

"He didn't know what was coming," I tell Patterson. "He had no idea, then he was dead."

Patterson nods with wide eyes.

I push past him into the bedroom. When I entered the room, I didn't see the blood between the bed and the wall.

"The female was found there," Patterson says quietly. "Probably drawn by the gunshot to her husband."

I look from Patterson to the door leading to the hall. He gets the point and steps out.

Kneeling by the blood, I say my prayer again and touch the sticky stain.

Surprise and fear. We didn't tell anyone. I swear we didn't. Please don't kill me. I shouldn't have asked for more. He shot Lane. Help. Mint and vanilla. Please don't.

The vision is fresh and sharp and leaves me shaking. On my knees I look to Patterson, "Do you smell that?"

"That's gun powder."

"No, the mint and vanilla? It's so strong."

He sniffs the air. "I don't smell it. Maybe Mr. Markle wore Aqua Velva?"

I suddenly have a memory of Father's Day gifts from my previous life. A blue bottle of cologne wrapped with love.

Nausea floods with the memory. "It's been in front of me the whole time," I moan. "The matching smells."

I push past Patterson and run down the stairs to find Lucas. Flattening myself against the wall, I shuffle past Dustin's bloodstain, then run into the front yard.

Lucas and Chief Simmons are deep in conversation. Simmons barks orders at a few officers who hurry to their cruisers.

I want to tell Lucas what I found out, I want to blurt, "He killed them all." I stop in the grass and snap my mouth closed.

Something is wrong.

Lucas feels my gaze on him.

"You done?" he asks gently, his body tense.

I nod. "Everything okay?" I eye a cruiser pulling away. "Where are they going?"

"We have another call. A woman is holding her husband hostage at gunpoint." He crosses the grass to take my hand. "We have to divert some men to the scene."

Another wave of guilt. "It's Ashley Gerber, isn't it?"

"How?"

"She just found out her husband is having an affair." I focus on the grass, on the toes of my hiking boots. Another dangerous mess I caused. More carnage because of me. "She's a client," I say miserably, and keep my insights about my father to myself.

Lucas exhales long and loud.

"I only told her what I saw," I plead for him to understand. "I had no idea she'd flip out and hold him at gunpoint."

"Go to the hospital," he finally says. "Sit with Grandma Dot and Alexis and pray for Dustin. That's the best thing you can do right now."

Guilt flips to worry. "He's going to be fine. He has to be."

"He will be, but he needs you there with the family. I have to stay here for now, but I'll catch up with you later at the hospital, okay?"

"Okay," I say weakly. He kisses me on the forehead and releases me to the night.

When I said 'okay,' I meant it.

When I climb into my Charger, I change my mind.

Sitting and worrying in a waiting room is not the best thing I can do right now.

Convincing myself that changing my mind about my destination isn't the same thing as lying to Lucas, I formulate my plan.

I have one stop to make first. One detail to nail down.

Chapter 28

Gabby

"Gabriella, where are you?" Grandma Dot yells, her voice so shrill, I hold the phone away to protect my ear. "You should be here."

"I know, I know." I can confront the chief of police and keep my courage, but Grandma Dot reduces me to a petulant teenager. "I have something to do."

"What could be more important than waiting for your brother to come out of surgery? He's fighting for his life and you're out doing who-knows-what."

"I was at the crime scene." I swallow hard. "Dad's alive. He shot Dustin, he killed Vee and Lane."

"Oh, my," Grandma breathes into the phone. "Emily's coming home."

"Chief Simmons is working on that right now."

"My baby girl will be free," she mutters, lost in her own emotions.

I hate to ruin the moment, but I need answers. "If I'm right, he also killed Crystal and Lucy." I pause, give her time to let the news sink in.

"Good heavens, how awful is this man? Have they caught him yet?"

"Not yet, but I'm working on it."

"You? You need to be here, not chasing a crazy murderer, even if he is your father." Her emotions are focused now, on protecting me.

I let her anger slide past me. "When I showed you that coin, you said you'd seen one once. Have you remembered where?"

"Gabriella, whatever this is, stay out of this. He's dangerous."

"I'm not staying out of it," I snap. Just answer the question. Where did you see the coin?"

"It was a long time ago," she hedges.

"So you do remember. I'll do this with or without your help. Please tell me."

She exhales long and loud. "When I packed up your parents' stuff. After …."

A memory flashes through my mind. A box of personal items that fell off a shelf. A photo album with pictures of my family. A jewelry box, its contents spilled across the carpet.

"I know where it is," I tell her.

"Gabriella, don't. Just stop."

"You know I can't stop now." My voice low and firm. "Hug Alexis for me and let her know my thoughts are there with you guys."

"Gabriella?"

I hang up on her and speed through the dark country roads. Grandma's farm is only a few miles away. My phone rings again but I ignore it.

A few moments later, it rings again.

"I'm not talking right now," I say to Grandma's number on the screen and toss the phone on the passenger seat.

Grandma's kitchen light spills onto the back porch, a welcoming beacon of home.

The bright light clashes with my dark mood.

I let myself into the kitchen and Jet barks, excited to see me. "Not now," I snap at him, pushing him off my legs. Jet cowers at the harsh words but follows me up the stairs to Grandma's bedroom.

High on her closet shelf, where I stuck it a few months ago, I find the box of things Grandma hid away after Mom was sent to prison. I pull it off the shelf and dump the contents on Grandma's bed. Papers and the photo album spread across the quilt. The album falls open to a picture of my dad.

I slam the album shut on his smiling, lying face.

"You don't deserve to be remembered like that," I say to the closed book.

I pull each drawer out of the jewelry box and add the assorted items to the pile on the quilt. Pushing away the bracelets and earrings and mementos, I find some coins. The gold coin sparkles amongst the pesos from a trip to Mexico when we were kids, a silver dollar, a flattened penny from the zoo.

"Gotcha," I shout to the room.

My mother's wedding ring catches my attention, the

same way it did the first time I went through this box.

I take off my right glove and slide the ring on my finger. It's a perfect fit.

Last time, I used the ring to feel closer to my mother.

Tonight it's a symbol of our revenge.

"Now you'll be there, too," I say to mom. "I'll bring him down for all of us."

Leaving the mess for later, I hurry back downstairs. Jet anxiously follows. I spare him a moment before I leave and rub him behind the ears. "Be a good boy until Grandma comes home, okay?"

He wags his tail at the attention and I leave him behind.

Grandma has called a few more times while I was inside. I ignore the many notifications of her voice mails and scroll through my contacts.

When I find the number I need, I type in my carefully crafted text.

"I know about the coins. I want to join you. Tell him to meet me where he met Crystal."

My fingers tingle as I hit send, hoping she'll take the bait.

I wait in my car behind Grandma's house for a response. Not sure I'll get one or if I'm wrong. A pile of dirt and gravel under the porch catches my eyes as I wait.

"Darn groundhogs," I mutter. "Grandma's going to shoot you if she sees you." I laugh with nervous tension, remembering spring afternoons watching Grandma shoot the pests with her .22 pistol.

I climb back out of my car and bound up the steps and

into the kitchen. Behind a collection of mismatched winter gloves and flashlights, I find the coffee can on the shelf in a closet. Grandma's pistol clanks heavily in the can, a scattering of bullets loose at the bottom.

The gun feels foreign in my hand. Grandma taught both Dustin and me to shoot when we were kids. Dustin took to it right away and loved shooting. I was always nervous with the power of the gun, even in the small .22.

Silently thanking Grandma for the lessons long ago, I fill the magazine with bullets and tuck the gun in the waistband of my jeans.

Jet looks at me curiously. "Just in case," I tell him.

My phone chirps a response to my text.

"OK."

"Here we go," I say to Jet and stride into the dark.

Chapter 29

Gabby

In the house that Deidre built, all the lights are on. The lovely home stands like a mask in the dark, the lighted windows eyes that hide the evil inside.

I drive past the house and park near the bridge the way I did the first time. In my haste, I forget about the drop-off on the side of the road. With a sinking feeling, I feel my front tire slide off the road.

My phone rings again and I snatch it angrily. "Grandma, stop calling! My tire just got stuck again and I don't have time for this."

"Gabby? What are you doing?"

It's not Grandma. It's Lucas. I freeze guiltily. "You don't want to know. Trust me, you don't want to know what's really going on here."

I hang up on the man I love, hating myself for leaving him out, but needing to protect him from the truth if I can. I power my phone off before he can call back.

"Just do what you need to do," I give myself a pep-talk and shut the door silently behind me. "He'll forgive you when this is all over."

Moonlight spills across the bridge, the eternal ripple of the river plays through the air. A sharp wind cuts against my face and I wrap my coat tighter.

The dark woods loom like a wall of menace. A shiver runs up my back and I zip up my collar. This deserted section of river was less than inviting in the daylight. The rising wind rattles through bare branches like the soundtrack from a horror movie.

"Crap on a cracker, get moving," I mutter and step off the road into the snow. The moon and stars overhead offer little light and I struggle over downed branches and slide on wet leaves. Keeping the river on my left, I push on and ignore my rising panic.

"Just call Lucas," my rational mind says.

"Not until you're sure about her involvement," the part of me desperate to protect him argues.

Even prepared for the sharp drop I slid down last time, the slippery snow wins against my feet and I slide down the hill. Snow shoves up the back of my coat and into the waist band of my pants. After landing with a huff, I check to make sure the gun is still secure.

The cold metal is firmly in place.

The putrid smell of death wrinkles my nose. I've slid into the rotten remains of a raccoon or some other furry woodland creature. It's insides are smeared on my jeans. With handfuls of snow, I wipe at the sick stain.

The largest globs of yuck wipe away, but a heavy scent of rotting flesh clings to my gloves.

I shake them off as best I can and make my way to the

clearing nestled on the riverbank.

The peeling paint of the shack stands out in the moonlight. The heart with Lucas loves Ka barely visible. The sagging roof line and leaning walls exude and air of desperation that matches my own. I lick my dry lips and the cold air wicks at the moisture. My entire body tingles, my muscles jumpy with excess adrenaline.

I touch the gun tucked into my jeans. Its presence offers no comfort. How had things gone so wrong that I'm meeting my dead father in a run-down shack in the woods with a gun in my pants?

If I wasn't so anxious, I'd find this funny.

Nothing about murder and betrayal is funny.

The snow in the clearing swirls in the wind, but is unmarred by footprints.

I'm the first one here.

Leaving tell-tale marks behind me, I go to the door of the shack. It hangs by the single hinge, the darkness behind it broken only by moonlight pouring through the holes in the roof. I wait outside the door for a few minutes, stomping my feet in the snow to keep them warm.

Another gust of winter air convinces me to enter. The stench inside is worse than the smell lingering on my glove.

As my eyes adjust to the dark, the wind mourns its way through the flimsy walls. The shack looks the same as before, only sadder, if possible. The destroyed mattress and broken chairs lurk in the corners. Plastic cups and empty beer cans skitter under my stomping feet.

"What are you doing out here?" I mutter to myself. "This is crazy."

My rational mind almost wins, almost convinces me to leave and go to the hospital where I belong, where it's warm, where my family waits.

Approaching voices keep me inside the shack, my ears straining to hear the words over the whistling wind.

"You sure this is where she said to meet?" Nathan, no longer Dad, asks.

"She said meet me where you met Crystal. This is where the accident happened, right?"

My heart sinks. I knew she'd be here. I knew she was guilty.

For Lucas' sake, I'd hoped I was wrong.

"Yeah," he says carefully.

"Then this must be where she meant," Deidre answers. "I don't want to be out here in this cold either. Look, there's her footprints. She's inside."

"Gabby?" Nathan calls.

Hearing my name from his lips knocks the air out of me. I gasp at the rush of emotions. I'd dreamed of this moment since I first saw him at the cemetery months ago. I'd dreamed of a happy reunion, of his strong arms surrounding me, of the words he'd say that would form an explanation of where he's been all these years.

The man I dreamed of was a figment of my imagination.

This man is a monster who kills for his benefit and shot his own son.

"Come out so I can see you," he says.

"Lord, let me say what I need to say," I pray silently, and step out of the shack.

"Man, it's good to see you," Nathan says with what sounds like actual excitement.

My mouth has gone dry, and I can only manage a, "Yep."

Deidre looks from me to him and back at me. "Your text said you wanted in on the coins."

I say, "Yep," again and add a nod.

Deidre laughs a little, "We stopped the coin thing years ago. Not long after the children discovered where we were storing them. Paying them off cut into our profits." She nods to the shack. "Guess you already knew about that. Gregor told me he found you snooping around out here."

"I was out here the other day," I concede.

"Told you she was good," Nathan says. His praise sits uncomfortably on me.

Deidre smiles wickedly, "We don't do the coins anymore. We only ship stronger stuff in the cars now. Are you okay with that?"

I finally find my voice and fain interest, "What kind of stronger stuff?"

"Whatever fits in the cars we sell overseas," Nathan supplies. "With your special talents, the sky's the limit on what we can make now."

"Is there a lot of money in it?" I push.

"Tons," he says simply. "So you're in?"

I pretend to seriously think it over. If he knew me at all, he'd know I'd never agree. "Is the money worth it?" I

233

ask finally.

"It pays lots better than being a grease monkey on fancy cars that I'd never be able to own."

"We're offering you money, power, prestige. Lots more than you have now with that little freak show you call a shop," Deidre says with a disturbing smile. "We have a shipment going out soon, and a few details to nail down first. Your help could be vital in making the deal even sweeter." In her expensive down coat and knee-high boots that cost as much as my car, she fairly glitters with greed.

My stomach churns with distaste and my hand balls into a fist at my side. Ignoring the smiling woman, I lock eyes on Nathan.

"I meant, was the money worth it to destroy your family?"

"Are you going to bring this up now? That was years ago." His calm dismissal stings.

"Right, years of Mom sitting in prison for murdering a man who is obviously not dead."

"I told you she wouldn't let that go." Deidre seems to enjoy our little family drama.

"You hit me in the head that night," I cry, losing my calm control. "You nearly killed me."

Deidre breaks into a loud, wild laugh that's carried on the harsh wind. "Him? He'd never hurt you on purpose."

I stare at the crazy woman, my mouth open in question.

"My dear, I'm the one who hit you. Nosey little brat, you should have stayed in your room." The sudden venom startles and nervous sweat drips down my rib cage.

"Deidre," Nathan snaps. "That's enough."

Deidre stops laughing and simpers, "Sorry, Nate." She bats her eyelashes and slithers around his arm in an overtly flirtatious manner. I lose even more respect for the man when he falls for it. She looks over her shoulder the way she did at the party with Lucas, claiming her victory.

Clinging to his arm, she asks, "So are you in or not?"

It's my turn to laugh, "Am I in? You really are crazy. I'd never join a group of murdering thieves."

Deidre's perfectly made up face falters a moment then she forces the smile back. "Murder is a strong word," she warns.

"One that fits. First Crystal, then Lucy, then Vee and Lane. Did you get tired of paying them all off so you took them out?"

Deidre stammers, "Vee and Lane are dead?" Her hair blows in a tumult around her face as she looks from me to Nathan and back. "Lucy was killed by her horse. And Crystal?" Her face crumples. "Crystal was an accident. You said it was an accident." She drops Nathan's arm and steps back in disgust.

"It was, I promise." He puts his hands up in defense.

I push my advantage, "The irony is so sweet," I say touching the scar on my eyebrow. "You hitting me gave me the talents that ultimately brought you down."

"It's not true," Deidre says to me. "You just want to turn me against him."

"Gabby, stop," Nathan says in a low growl.

I have no intention of stopping now. "With all your

money, you still wear cheap drugstore cologne. I smelled it in my visions of all the bodies you left behind." Shivers of rage run up my legs and down my arms.

His mouth drops open in surprise, then curls into a sick smile. "Wearing the cologne reminds me of you kids. Believe it or not, I've missed you and Dustin. I've been closer than you think this whole time." A wistful look crosses his face. "You put all that together based on what cologne I wear? Come on, we can be rolling in cash if you're on the team."

I've heard enough. I snatch the gun from my pants and point it at his chest. "I'll never help you!" I scream, spittle dribbling down my chin. "I'd rather die than help you hurt anyone else."

"Nathan, Crystal?" Deidre croaks, oblivious to my drawn gun. "She's lying, right?"

"Of course, babe. I explained it all to you that day," he soothes Deidre. With hands raised, he tells me, "Okay, calm down. You hate me, I get it."

My hands shake on the gun, and I clench the handle tighter. Mom's ring pushes uncomfortably into my finger. "Don't tell me to calm down," I snap. "Stop. Just stop right there."

"We both know you won't shoot me," he says, his frustrating calm back in full force.

"I will." The violent shaking of my hands gives me away. "Don't come any closer."

"What's the plan here, Gabby?" He's so close, I can smell the Aqua Velva.

I draw a blank, not sure what grand idea I thought I'd

come up with if it reached this point.

"Make you turn yourselves in," I stammer. "Face what you've done."

Disappointment washes over his face, and a gun suddenly appears in his hand glinting in the moonlight.

I stare stupidly at the barrel directed at me. Terror courses through my body, freezing me in place. He shot Dustin with this same gun a few hours ago. He'll shoot me now and I'll die alone here in the woods. I look to Deidre for help, but mollified by Nathan's lies, she's once again enjoying our drama.

"Don't, please don't," I whimper miserably. My chin quivers so badly, my teeth chatter. I cock my .22, knowing it's not match for his larger gun, knowing I won't be able to shoot him.

Desperately, I think of my tattoo, beg it for an answer.

My tattoo is silent.

"Just shoot the liar, Nate," Deidre coos into the wind.

"We need her," Nathan argues.

"Don't go soft now. We've done just fine without her," she urges. "I'll make it up to you." Her blatant romantic enticement over my possible murder makes me sick. Poor Lucas and Gregor, this woman is demented. I shift my aim to Deidre.

I could end this with a pull of my trigger. My finger itches to squeeze.

As disgusting as her true self is, I can't do that to Lucas.

The wind howls around us, gusts against my body, carries the scent of dead raccoon on my glove to my nose.

The shack creaks against the strain. A snapping board cracks into the night like a gunshot.

Nathan and Deidre turn their heads.

It's the advantage I need.

With my gun, I smack the larger gun out of Nathan's hand. It flops into the snow.

I don't wait for his reaction.

I run.

Chapter 30

GABBY

Nathan's longer legs reach me after only a few steps. He pushes me towards the riverbank, then tackles.

Ice at the edge of the river slices at my cheeks.

Desperately, I scramble. Only manage to go farther into the river.

The ice breaks and freezing water envelopes my face.

I wriggle onto my back, gasping air, and push with my legs to escape.

Nathan straddles my body, his hands on my throat.

Water soaks into my coat, the weight of the soggy material pulling me down as Nathan pushes me under.

Air. I need air.

The similarities to the vision from Crystal flow through me. The line between what happened to her and what's happening to me blurs.

The monster in both is the same.

I claw at his face with one hand and the pressure blessedly releases.

"What's that smell?" he howls.

"Finish her," Deidre cheers.

Behind his shoulder, I see the heart spray-painted on the side of the shack. "Lucas loves ...."

"Lucas, help me," I think desperately. "Lucas, please."

Nathan tightens his grasp on my throat and pushes me under again.

Splashing and gurgling, I swing wildly with the gun still in my hand. It bounces ineffectively off his shoulder.

The gun can serve a better use.

I wriggle against the pressure of his body on mine until I can point the gun at his belly.

Pull the trigger and it's all over.

I can't pull the trigger. I want to, I need to.

The cross tattoo on my arm screams into life, the intensity stronger than the stinging embrace of the icy water.

Drop the gun and play dead.

"Or pull the trigger," I argue in my mind.

DROP THE GUN AND PLAY DEAD.

I've never disobeyed the words God tells me through the tattoo before.

I obey them now.

I toss the gun and force myself to go slack.

He pushes me deeper underwater. I stay still.

He shoves until my head grinds into the river bottom. I stay still.

He lets go of my neck. I stay still.

He climbs off me and out of the river. I spring to life.

Gasping and crawling through the ice and snow, I wrap my hand around his ankle. A hard pull and he hits the ground, his face in the snow.

Deidre squeals.

I shove my putrid-smelling glove over his mouth, pummel him with my other fist.

He pries at my fingers, squirms and kicks.

I wrap my arm around him to keep my hand over his mouth, search the ground for a weapon.

My wet gloved fingers find a chunk of ice.

"Not so fun when you can't breathe," I hiss near his ear. "Now you know how Crystal felt."

Deidre shouts, "Stop," as I lift the block of ice high.

I don't stop, I slam it into his head.

The ice shatters.

Nathan stops struggling.

"I should have killed you when I had the chance years ago," Deidre screams.

I roll off Nathan's still body into the snow.

Framed by the moon overhead, her blond hair blowing in the wind, Deidre points the gun directly at my chest.

"You don't want to do this," I plead. "Think of Lucas. He loves me. You'll break his heart."

"Nate loves me. That didn't stop you," she argues.

"Please, Deidre, just drop the gun. We can work this out."

"There's nothing left to work out. You've ruined everything," she wails. "Nate?" She toes his side with her expensive boot. "Nate, baby?"

He either moans in response, or it's the wind.

"He's not worth it, Deidre," I say as calmly as possible with her gun pointed at me. "He killed Crystal."

"He said he didn't," she stammers. "He said it was an accident. He wouldn't lie to me."

A deep chill from my soaking clothes makes my teeth chatter. "He lied. That's what he does."

"Not to me. He said he loved me."

She sounds so pitiful, I almost feel sorry for her. A shudder wracks my body and I jerk in the snow.

"Gregor loves you too," I push, my teeth chattering. "Lucas loves you. Just drop the gun before you do something you'll regret."

Her sorrowful expression is chased away by her fake smile and empty eyes. "I only regret leaving you alive that night."

I try to crawl away, but my limbs won't listen, are heavy with cold. "D-d-d-Deidre, please."

My wet hair blows against my face, ice crystals scratching my skin.

"D-d-d-Deidre," she laughs. "Poor girl. Are you cold?"

"Drop the g-g-gun." Another shudder shakes me. I try to raise a hand in defense against the crazy woman. My arm moves in slow motion.

She looms over me, hair blowing wildly. "Don't worry about Lucas, dear. He'll never know I was here. Too bad you and Nate had such an awful fight."

My frozen lips struggle to form words. "D-d-drop it."

"Drop the gun!" The familiar male voice shouts into the clearing. "Drop it now."

Deidre spins in shock, I sink into the snow in relief.

"Lucas, dear. What are you doing here?" she asks in a completely different voice, sounding like a hostess at a party.

Lucas steps into the moonlight, his gun trained on his mother, his eyes darting around the scene. "What's going on here?"

"Just a friendly dispute with your girlfriend and her dad," Deidre tries.

"If it's friendly, lose the gun," he barks.

Deidre sets the gun prettily in the snow. "I was just trying to help Gabby," Deidre lies. "She and Nathan had an argument. She hit him in the head."

"That's Nathan McAllister?"

Deidre doesn't answer and my frozen lips won't make the words.

Lucas picks up Deidre's gun then kneels next to me. "Gabby, are you hurt?" His hands roam my body looking for injuries. My mind is sluggish and I can't focus my eyes.

"She got a little wet. This cold isn't good for her."

Lucas strips off my wet coat, then take off his. The coat is warm from his body, and the heat penetrates my chill enough so I can speak.

"Arrest her," I mutter, sitting up.

"Now, Gabby, what an awful thing to say," Deidre protests. "She must be delirious."

Lucas searches my face. I put all my emotions into my expression.

Confused, he decides to trust me.

"I don't know what's going on here, but you're lying about it and you had a gun on Gabby. Put your hands behind your back."

"Lucas, no," she pouts, backing away. "You can't arrest me."

"I'm just detaining you for now."

"I won't let you. I'm your mother." She continues backing away, her eyes desperate.

"Which is why I'm being polite instead of just cuffing you when I got here. Now give me your hands."

Deidre spins and attempts to run.

She plows into the side of the shack and bounces off.

The shack shudders at the impact.

Lucas grabs her wrist and wrangles it behind her back.

The shack strains against the howling wind.

The old wood creaks and moans. Slowly, the rotten building leans, shakes. Cracks of breaking wood fill the air. All at once, the shack gives up and crashes to the ground like a pile of broken bones.

A whoosh of putrid air flows out, the stench of years of neglect released from the decrepit walls.

The three of us stare in shock.

"Holy crap," Deidre says.

"That shack was bound to come down sometime," Lucas says.

"Not the shack," Deidre says. "Nate is gone."

The shape his body left in the snow lies empty like a snow angel. Footprints fade into the woods.

Lucas runs a few steps into the woods, following the trail.

"Don't," I manage to say loud enough to stop him.

Lucas notices my chattering and shivering under his dry coat. "We need to get you out of here," he says, picking me up and cradling me against his chest. "Mom, don't try anything stupid and come with me."

I hate that Lucas has to carry me.

I hate that he had to arrest his own mother.

I hate that Nathan got away again.

With my head lolling against Lucas' shoulder, a single thought keeps me warm.

My mother will be coming home.

After placing me in the front seat of his cruiser and buckling me in, Lucas opens the back door for Deidre. She squeezes into the cramped seat, muttering her distaste.

If you don't like being arrested, you shouldn't have become a criminal.

He starts the car and cranks the heat. "Good thing you said your tire was stuck again," he says nodding to my Charger parked awkwardly on the side of the road. "Or I wouldn't have known where to find you."

"Sorry about that," I mutter against my shivers.

"You have to stop running into trouble on your own. I'm always here to help." He glances in the rear-view mirror at his mom. "And you, what the heck is going on here?"

"I don't want to talk about it," she pouts prettily. "It's all a misunderstanding."

I yearn to shout about all her 'misunderstandings' but this isn't the place. Lucas will get the whole story soon enough.

"Can you take me home?" I ask.

"You mean to the hospital?"

"I am going to the hospital, but only for Dustin. I just need a shower and some dry clothes first."

Thinking of Dustin sobers us instantly.

"What happened to Dustin?" Deidre asks.

Is it possible she doesn't know? My anger heats me up. "Nathan shot him tonight. Dustin interrupted the murder of Vee and Lane Markle and was shot for his troubles," I say.

"Oh, my. You were serious when you said that? I thought you were trying to trick us."

"I'm not a liar, like you," I snap. Lucas puts his hand on top of mine. "Sorry," I say again.

We drive into town and through River Bend in silence. Questions in all of our heads. As we turn onto my street, Deidre finally asks. "Did he really kill Crystal?"

She sounds earnest. For the first time since becoming reacquainted with her, she feels like a real woman.

"He did." The simple honest truth.

Lucas parks in front of my house, my vandalized and scratched garage door bright in his headlights. I open my door and pull off his coat. "You two need to talk. I'm going to shower and change real quick. Then we'll go see about Dustin."

I shut the door before Lucas can argue.

They have lots to talk about and don't need an audience.

What I need is to be warm and dry, Grandma Dot telling me it will all be okay, and Dustin safely out of surgery.

Chapter 31

Gabby

A fresh blanket of snow covers the cemetery, crisp and white and sparkling in the morning sunshine. The tent over our heads rattles with a forlorn sound.

A line of officers, resplendent in their dress blues, stands nearby. The colorful finery contrasts brightly against the new snow.

Grandma Dot sinks into the chair next to me in the front row and takes my hand. Her reassuring squeeze is meant to calm. Her firm grip an anchor against the tide of swirling emotions.

"Dustin would love this," she says quietly, nodding to the American flag draped on the coffin suspended over the open grave.

"The flowers are lovely, too," I mutter pointlessly. "Many from his station."

Further down the row, a child's cry pierces the hushed scene. Alexis puts Walker on her shoulder and bounces with the easy grace of motherhood. Walker shoves his face into her neck, wraps her hair around his pudgy fingers, and settles.

I envy his quick recovery from tears to calm.

Envy his lack of understanding about why we are here at this cemetery this morning.

I scan the gathering crowd for a familiar face, and spot Lucas talking to a group of fellow officers. His dress blue uniform sets off the blue in the eyes that meet mine across the crowd. He gives me a reassuring half-smile and a nod.

It's what I needed at this moment.

Goosebumps dot my bare legs. It's the third occasion I've had to wear the blue sweater dress Grandma bought me.

My least favorite occasion of the three.

"You cold?" my mom, Emily, asks. "You have goose bumps."

I'm not used to hearing her voice in real life. Not used to the freedom to touch her hand. I take that hand in mine. Try not to think about how thin she feels.

She's home with us now.

"I'm good," I reply. "Not a great event for you to come home to."

"No, it's not," she says softly. She releases my hand and puts her arm around my shoulders. She runs her fingers through my curls. I lean into her shoulder and drink in the moment.

She's home with us now.

At the far edge of the cemetery, a news van parks. "Lacey and her crew are here," I say to Grandma Dot.

"She better leave you alone until this is over," Grandma replies with narrowed eyes. "This is a family matter."

I swallow hard and clench a fist against my thigh. "Family matter," I repeat.

The seats under the tent fill up and a crowd of people forms a swarm around us. "Good turn out," Alexis says, patting Walker on the back. "Dustin would be pleased." Her eyes slide away from the coffin and drift to the waiting hearse with its dark windows. She stares at the hearse with eyes worn from worry.

Scanning the crowd again, I find Lucas and give him a tight smile. I wish he could be sitting here with me, but he takes his position in the line of officers next to Chief Simmons.

The pastor from Grandma's church steps forward as the last few stragglers join the group of mourners. A hush settles over the crowd.

I swallow hard again and focus on my breathing to stay calm. The pastor begins speaking and I run my hands down my thighs nervously.

My tattoo begins to tingle and I snap my gaze to Lucas.

He's been watching me intently, ready.

As the pastor continues speaking, Lucas steps away from the formal line of officers and into the crowd of mourners.

My eyes follow him, but from my seat at the front of the service, I can't see over the crush of people.

I grab both Grandma Dot and Mom's hands and

squeeze hard.

"Nathan McAllister, put your hands up." Lucas barks over the pastor's calm voice.

"We got him," I bubble with excitement. "We got him."

I push through the crowd of plain-clothed officers. He's dyed his hair and shaved his beard in an attempt to disguise himself. When we thought he was dead, it was easy for him to sneak into Dustin's basketball games and other important moments in our lives.

Today we were all on the lookout.

Nathan attempts to run, dashes around the gravestones.

Lucas is right behind him, and I'm only a few steps behind.

Nathan trips over a pile of uneven dirt hidden under the snow, remnants from the exhumation of Crystal. I picked this location on purpose.

Lucas is on him before he can wriggle away.

I jump onto the pile, unable to stop myself.

Lucas gets one of Nathan's wrists twisted behind his back and I pull the other wrist. A circle of plain-clothed officers surrounds us, in on the ruse.

Someone sniggers at my involvement.

"Quite a girl you got there, Hartley."

I don't care if they make fun of me. I don't care if this should be done by the police.

The whole plan to catch him was my idea. I wouldn't miss it.

Lucas straddles Nathans back, holding his wrists in

place. I stand and put my foot on his neck the way I've seen officers do on TV. Nathan's umph of pain fills me with sick satisfaction.

"I knew you wouldn't miss Dustin's funeral," I hiss at the man.

"Gabby," he says, gasping against my dress shoe on the side of his neck. "I'm so sorry about your brother."

The swirl of my emotions bubble into a frenzy. "It's your fault he got shot," I snap. "It's your fault for all of this."

"I never meant for him to die," he says miserably.

I enjoy his misery. "Hurts thinking someone you love is dead, doesn't it?"

His face fills with confusion.

"You've only had a few days to feel that way. Dustin and I have spent years missing you. Grieving for you. Now it's over."

I shout over my shoulder at the waiting hearse. "Dustin, do you have something you want to say to our dear father?"

Dustin climbs out of the vehicle and joins us with a smug smile.

"I do have something to say." With one arm in a sling, he takes handcuffs from his pocket with his good arm. "Nathan McAllister, you're under arrest." With Lucas' help, Dustin roughly cuffs him, stands him up, then pushes him to Chief Simmons. "Chief, get this piece of trash out of here."

Nathan gapes at the crowd surrounding him. "This was all a setup?" he asks dumbly. "You faked a funeral?"

"Faking deaths must run in the family," I retort.

Chief Simmons pulls Nathan by the cuffs, grumbling, "Come on."

"Chief, wait," Grandma Dot shouts, pushing through the officers to face Nathan. Her fist connects with his jaw before anyone can stop her. "That's for Emily," she hisses.

Cuffed and unable to defend himself, Nathan stumbles backwards and falls on his back in the snow. Grandma kicks him in the ribs. "This if for Gabby." She kicks him again. "This is for Dustin."

Nathan rolls on his back like a turtle on its shell. "Are you going to stop her?" he demands of Chief Simmons.

The chief says to Grandma, "One more, then that's enough."

Relishing the moment, Grandma sinks a final kick into him. "That's for taking my daughter from me."

The chief drags Nathan to his feet once again.

"You want to get one in, too, Emily?" the chief asks Mom.

My mother smiles sweetly, wraps her arm around Grandma's shoulder. "I think my mom took care of it just fine."

"You are all crazy," Nathan shouts as he's drug away. "A fake funeral? You're nuts."

He continues to squall until he's loaded into a cruiser.

"Did you hurt yourself?" I ask Grandma Dot.

She shakes her foot and rubs her knuckles. "Only a little. It was worth it."

Lucas slides his arm around my waist. "You okay?"

"I'm great," I answer honestly. "As long as we never

actually go to Dustin's funeral."

"Ha!" Dustin laughs. "I'm going to outlive all of you."

"You better," Alexis chimes in, handing Walker to Dustin. "Even pretending you were dead was awful."

"I kind of enjoyed it," Dustin says. "You all looked so sad, made me feel important."

"Acting. We were all acting," I say.

From the news van parked at the edge of the cemetery, Lacey Aniston walks towards us.

"Crap on a cracker, time to pay the piper," I grumble. "She did fake a report on Dustin's untimely demise for us. Now I owe her an interview."

"Just do like I do and say no comment," Dustin offers.

"I promised a comment." I force a smile and walk across the snow to meet Lacey.

"You ready for our interview now?" Lacey asks.

"Ready as I'll ever be."

"This story will for sure clinch my spot at the Indianapolis station. Heck, I might even try for a job in Chicago," Lacey chatters.

If this interview helps get Lacey out of River Bend, I'm all for it. "What do you want to know?"

"Mistletoe, Daddy," Olivia says, pointing to the green sprig hanging above Lucas and me at Grandma Dot's. "You have to kiss Gabby."

"Well, if you say so, Ollie-bug." Lucas pulls me close and plants a quick peck on my lips.

"Ooh, gross," Olivia giggles and runs to the Christmas tree.

"I'll give you a better one later," he says so only I can hear.

"Get a room," Dustin grumbles good-naturedly, slapping Lucas on the shoulder. "Olivia's right, gross."

"Good thing you're in a sling, or I'd smack you," I tease my brother, then follow him into the living room to join the family around the Christmas tree.

"The psychological effects of incarceration on the human mind is fascinating," Gregor Hartley is saying to Mom. She wears a polite smile, but is obviously uncomfortable.

"Save her," I mouth to Lucas.

"Dad, would you like another drink?" Lucas interrupts.

"I'd love some more iced tea. Dot, this tea is delicious," Gregor says.

"Come on, Dad," Lucas says. "I'll help you in the kitchen."

I settle into the empty seat next to Mom on the couch. "Thank you," she breathes. "Poor man. I feel sorry for him, but boy he can talk."

I snuggle closer and say, "You get used to it after a while."

"Now, that son of his," Mom teases.

"Gabriella did good there," Grandma chimes in. "Both the kids chose well," she adds, smiling at Alexis and Dustin.

"Is it time yet?" Olivia asks Lucas when he returns to the living room. "Grandma Dot said Walker and I could open a present tonight."

"It's only Christmas Eve, so just one," Grandma says.

Her face glows with joy.

She finally got her most treasured wish, her whole family together for the holidays.

I got the best present of all, a room full of people who love and accept me exactly as I am.

THE END

Want another great book to read? Try these other small town murder mysteries by Dawn Merriman, available on Amazon. You can also see all Dawn Merriman's books, and join her personal newsletter to receive a FREE short story at DawnMerriman.com

Marked by Darkness
Maddison, Indiana – Book 1

An intensely emotional, psychological thriller. Consumed with grief from losing her husband and children, Maribeth lives alone in a cabin in the woods. Haunted by her dead family and the choices that destroyed them, she just wants to heal. When a woman is murdered and left in her woods, Maribeth can no longer hide. The serial killer who destroyed her life has a copy cat determined to finish her off.

Inheriting Elyse
Maddison, Indiana – Book 2
Heart-breaking and heart-pounding supernatural thriller. After a crushing family tragedy, Melinda inherits her aunt's farm in Maddison, Indiana. The farm was once lovely, but her aunt was a hoarder and the house is packed with boxes, toys and dolls. Lots of dolls. Even hoarded, the farm should be the perfect place for her family to heal and rebuild. Melinda, her husband and teenage step-daughter soon realize they've inherited more than the farm. As they clear the house of boxes, their true inheritance is released. Can Melinda's mind survive the legacy left to her? Can her family?

Field of Flies
Two people want Zoey, dead. One is in her own mind. A quiet, emotionally distressed, pig farmer is sucked into a murder investigation. But closing in on a killer is dangerous. Which is worse - a killer desperate to keep her from finding the truth - or the killer in her mind. Maybe she can stop them both….

If you missed the first two books in this series, read them now.

Message in the Bones – Book 1
Message in the Fire – Book 2

A note from Dawn Merriman,

Crap on a cracker, Gabby has come a long way from the lonely woman being made fun of at the coffee shop at the beginning of Book 1. It has been an honor to chronicle her journey and tell her story. She may have more adventures ahead of her at some point in the future, but I'm glad she is happy and has some answers for now. I hope I did Gabby justice. Thank you for following this adventure with me. My fans are the best in the world!

I can't tell these stories without a great support team. The ending of this third novel had me stuck so many times, I really needed the support! As always, my husband is the best. He's spent so many hours hashing over plot details with me, I can never thank him enough. Just venting to him about a part that has me stuck gets my creativity flowing and his questions let me see things from a different point of view.

My teenage son has been at home with me during the writing of this book and was assaulted with my angst over the tricky ending of this series. Thank you, Chase, for your honest comments and suggestions.

My beta readers really got a workout on this project. I ultimately wrote several versions of the ending and each of them patiently read them, then the next version, then discussed the merits of each, etc. Huge thank you to Lori Ream and her long conversations with me. She may know these characters better than I do at this point. Katie and Liz, your input was so helpful as always.

Leaving Gabby behind is bittersweet. I love all these characters and am sad to say good-bye. I'm also excited about future projects that have been swirling around in the back of my mind and want to be told.

I love hearing from fans. Please follow me and find out first about new books or interact with me on various topics by signing up for my newsletter at DawnMerriman.com. You can also e-mail me directly at DawnMerrimanNewsletter@gmail.com.

If you have enjoyed any of my books, please leave a review. Reviews are very helpful to us authors.

As I've mentioned before, listening to music is a HUGE inspiration while I write. Here are a few songs that made a big impact on this book. Please support these artists.

Bloodstream, by Ed Sheeran (Gabby's theme song)
You, by Candlebox
(Don't fear) the Reaper, by Blue Oyster Cult
A Fifth of Beethoven, by Walter Murphy
The Final Countdown, by Europe
God Made a Woman, by Lauren Mascitti
To Make You Feel My Love, by Bob Dylan

A truly heartfelt thank you to all my fans and my team. Without you, I'm just a woman spending way too much time typing.

God Bless,
Dawn Merriman